Second Chance
DETOUR

ON THE ROAD TO LOVE SERIES

USA TODAY BESTSELLING AUTHOR

Verlene Landon

COPYRIGHT

Second Chance Detour
Verlene Landon
Copyright © 2019 Verlene Landon - Rusty Halo Books
All rights reserved.

Editing: My Brother's Editor
Cover Design: Bookend Designs
Cover Photographer: Wander Aguiar
Cover Model: Chaun W.

Publisher's Note:
No part of this book may be reproduced, scanned, or distributed in any printed or electronic form without express written permission from the publisher. The scanning, uploading, and distribution of this book via the Internet or any other means without the permission of the publisher is illegal and punishable by law. Please do not participate in or encourage piracy of copyrighted materials in violation of the author's rights. Purchase only authorized editions.

Without limiting the rights under copyright reserved above, no part of this publication may be reproduced, resold (as a "used" e-book), stored or introduced into a retrieval system, or transmitted, in any form or by any means (electronic, mechanical, photocopying, recording or otherwise), without prior written permission of both the copyright owner and the above publisher of this book.

This book is a work of fiction. People, places, events, and situations are the product of the author's imagination. Any resemblance to actual persons, living, dead, undead, immortal, or living in a douche-like state, or historical events, is purely coincidental.

ISBN: 978-0998126777

JUST SO YOU KNOW

This book contains adult themes, situations, and language.

There are also situations which some readers might find disturbing or triggering.

Within these pages you may find scenes that may depict, mention, or discuss: cheating, miscarriage, and more.

(But you will also find first loves who find a second chance at a roadside motel with shag carpet and meddling owners.)

If you need or desire more in-depth information to make an informed choice, visit VerleneLandon.com/OTRTL2

This book is for anyone who got stranded because they snapped a U joint and dropped a drive shaft.

CHAPTER 1

"Shit." Ben cursed in his typical fashion. No matter how much had changed since they'd been R & B, some things never did. Like the way his sharp jawline looked even more razor-like when he was pissed. Or how his one deep dimple seemed so bottomless when he was smiling cynically. Rayna missed being the R in the couple that used to be R & B, but there was nothing she could do about that now.

The only reason he was even tolerating her presence was for their mutual benefit, and not the sexy naked fun kind either. Those thoughts would get her nowhere quick, but her heart wanted what it wanted. *Only one surefire way to shut that traitorous organ up.*

She reached into the driver's side window to her purse on the seat and unzipped it. She checked to make sure Ben wasn't looking before she stuck her fingers into the one compartment no one else would dare go, the one with tampons and pads. That dark and mysterious pocket was no-man's-land.

Looking back once more to confirm he was still occupied with his phone, she retrieved a worn scrap of photo paper. She never understood why she'd printed the damn thing out instead of just deleting it off her phone along with the sender's number. Maybe a part of her liked being the victim; it made her role in their demise a touch easier to swallow.

When she looked down at the unfolded image, she felt the pain anew and remembered all the denial. Everything came flooding back as if it were happening in live action.

Of course, she wasn't there, but she imagined the picture as a video. She could hear those sexy little groans Ben always made whenever she nibbled his ears or lazily caressed his nipple. Those were two of his favorite spots. There and the underside of his highly developed V muscle, but it wasn't her making his eyes close in ecstasy with her lips at his ear. It was Treena—super-mega-whore, Treena.

Treena naked in his bed with her perfect breasts pushed up against his bicep. Super-mega-whore's toned leg bent across Ben's impeccable cock, hidden only by a sheet. His torso on display in all its *I was-sculpted-by-a-master* glory. His neck arched back, those dark, seductive eyes shuttered in bliss while she nibbled his ear. *The ear I should've been nibbling.*

Of course, in her head, the video extended beyond what the picture captured. When he'd had enough teasing, he'd have tossed Treena on her whore back and fucked her into next week. She could hear his pleasure and practically see his O face. *Ugh, how did I think we could pull this off? Ben wants nothing to do with me beyond this ruse, and all I see when I look at him is betrayal.*

"Well, all is not ruined. I pushed my meeting to Thursday, so we have time to get the car fixed and visit your dad before we need to take off. Hey, what do you have there, Ray?" As startled as she was by his sudden presence behind her, hearing the familiar version of her name from his lips for the first time since they broke up damn near did her in.

This whole ridiculous arrangement was a mistake. Fooling her family into believing they were still together was one thing. If they failed at that, well, it just meant hurt feelings and disappointment.

If Ben failed to secure the contract to manage this up-and-coming star in the world of football as his first big client, he was out of a job.

The only info he had to go on was this guy fired his last manager because of a string of girlfriends who ended up in the rags with accusations of physical abuse. Of course, the link to his manager made *him* look bad, so he wanted someone settled but not old.

Fresh and family—that was where Rayna came in. But now hearing her nickname made it near impossible to pretend without ripping her heart out.

"Oh, nothing important, *Benton*." Emphasizing his name, she shoved the picture back in its hiding spot and closed her purse, then tossed it back on the seat for good measure. The pepper she put on his name wasn't her being petty—she was sure he thought so, though. He'd caught her off balance; this trip was so much harder on her than she'd expected.

She'd jumped at the chance to spend time with him, but when he'd proposed it as a business arrangement, she got into that mindset. It wounded like a bitch, but she did it. She owed him the help, even though he was the one who cheated. She'd ultimately started pushing him away before he strayed, and then she had insisted *he* atone when she had no proof at the time. No, that proof came later, after they were done in under her accusations and insecurities…*which I had valid reasons for, apparently.*

When she turned to Ben, everything in the picture faded, and she wanted nothing more than to fall into his arms. He would confess and beg forgiveness, and she would happily give it. It was a one-time indiscretion under the influence of pain meds, right? They were young and, well, isn't that what youth is for, making mistakes and learning from them?

"Sorry, *Rayna*. Habit, but if we're going to fool your parents and my potential client, we can't be that formal. So, if I mess up here and there, do you think you can let it go?" She noticed his hand rise and then drop back down. Almost as if he wanted to touch her cheek the way he used to, but that was her imagination. The set of his jaw said more than his words.

To anyone else, his words would sound like a plea, and they kind of were, but she knew the edge to them. *Can you just let it go, already? If you're not going to believe me, can you at least just let it go? The more you hold onto it, the more it reminds me you can't trust me.* Those were words he'd spoken more times than she cared to count. So while his tone seemed amicable, it was barbed.

"Of course, I can. Sorry, but you wanted it business, and I'm trying really hard to keep it that way. No matter what happened, you know how much I love you, so the names are simply a small concession that help me." If she wasn't mistaken, Ben's eyes flared at her confession. Of course, it was probably anger and not a flash of hope.

"I apologize for saying that. I should've kept that to myself, but I'll never apologize for feeling it." Rayna wiped her hands along her cotton-covered hips. "Ah, look, your salvation from this uncomfortable situation has come in the form of a burly guy in a red wrecker."

She pushed past him to walk toward the truck. Not that she was needed for that, but she had to get away—same thing.

"Ray…" Ben didn't bother finishing. He sounded defeated, and it was keeping her off balance. She thought he'd follow and try to pursue whatever conversation had been about to take place, but his phone buzzed again and he dropped his shoulders and raised it to his ear.

"Hi, I'm Rayna Wilson, and you are…my salvation."

Bud, according to his shirt, blushed. "I don't know about that, ma'am, but I'll do my best. So what happened to her?"

Rayna wished she could've given a better description than "it shook, made some metal sounds, and then just decided not to go," but she and Ben had been talking about every inane thing under the sun to avoid serious conversation, and her mind had drifted to pulling over and straddling his sculpted thighs. "It's supposed to go, and well, it doesn't. So other than a little shaking and some metallic sounds, I don't have much to offer, but can you fix it?"

Bud made his way to the car, took one look underneath, and nodded. "Looks like you snapped a U joint and dropped her driveshaft. That's good news and bad news."

"Oh no, tell me the good news is to my wallet because I am a little strapped here."

"Yes, ma'am. The cost shouldn't break your bank, but it may take a little bit to get the part. I can head over to Yarborough's Salvage Yard, and if he has a driveshaft sitting out there, it'll save you some money and some time. But, if he doesn't, well, it'll take me a few days to get the part in and get her fixed up for you, especially with the holiday. I'll get her back to the garage, and we'll go from there. Do you and your husband need a ride somewhere?"

"Oh, he's not my husband, but I guess we'll need to go somewhere. Any suggestions?" Rayna wasn't thrilled with the idea of being stuck with a frustrated Benton, but she couldn't say she would hate having a nice dinner with him or something while Bud worked on her piece of shit. "But, I'm on a pretty tight budget, so no place too expensive."

Bud chuckled. "I feel you, Miss Wilson, but I know of a little place that's run by good folks and it's reasonable and clean. No matter if Yarborough has the part, I can't possibly get her up and running before the morning after next, so you'll need a place for a few nights." Bud slid under the car, hooked a strap to something, and walked to the levers on the back of his truck. Rayna followed.

Shit, I may not even have the credit to pay for the repair, much less rooms for both of us. The thought that Ben could tolerate sharing a room with her was fleeting. Even with two beds, Ben would probably prostitute himself if it meant getting away from her. But there was zero chance he had the money to afford another room, so he would have no choice.

Bud nodded toward the car. "Go ahead and grab what you need from the car before I get it loaded."

Rayna snagged her purse through the driver's window, and by the time she made it around to the back, Ben had their bags out. Bud took them and put them behind the seat in the cab of the truck. "Well, folks, hop on in, and we'll get moving in just a few."

Ben helped her up into the truck then followed. Her breath hitched as his powerful thigh pressed into hers. His crisp, woodsy scent invaded her senses. Every bit of anger she still clung to melted away along with the eleven months and three days they'd been apart. "Ben—"

Her words were cut off as Bud suddenly appeared in the cab. "We're all set. I'll drive over to Chance Inn before heading to the garage. I'll give you a call as soon as I have something to tell you, but everything is likely closed tomorrow."

With that, he fired up the engine for the long, silent ride to their unplanned detour.

Unplanned, but not unwelcomed?

Ray blushed when Shakira's voice came through the crackly speakers of the tow truck. Bud was humming along and tapping his fingers on the steering wheel. She stole a glance at Ben. *Busted.* She blushed when he raised an eyebrow and winked. It was a song they knew well, and naughty memories came flooding back.

Quickly, she averted her gaze and prayed for the ride to end soon. When they turned on 2nd Avenue, Rayna's mind started spinning.

Chance Inn, 2nd Avenue.
Chance Inn, 2nd Avenue.
Chance on 2nd. . .second chance.

Rayna hadn't always believed in signs or fate, but things changed. People changed. And if a fake relationship, a dropped drive shaft, and an aptly named hotel weren't signs, she didn't know what was.

Could this unexpected detour be a second chance for them? A second chance for Ben to confess so they could move on…together.

If she could forgive him for cheating, surely, he could forgive her for the way she'd treated him toward the end. The things she'd done…said.

They arrived at the inn around dusk. It looked more like a roadside motel than an *inn*.

"Here we are. Sam and Megan are in the process of updating it and making it cozier, but either way, the rooms are clean, and they're good people."

In the waning light, Rayna could tell some of it had seen better days, but a lot of it looked fairly fresh. *Well, beggars can't be choosers.* Rayna hoped she could afford one of the updated rooms. She also sent up a silent prayer there would be limited availability so she could set her hastily thought up plan into motion.

They exited the truck and Bud pulled away as they approached the office. Ben caught her hand. "I'm sorry, Ray. I don't have…I mean…I'll pay you back." Rayna could see the pain on his face about not being able to pay his share. It was hard to see him that way. Benton was a proud man.

"No worries. I know you're good for it." Rayna tried not to make a big deal out of it either way. The less interested in the money she appeared, the more it would put him at ease.

"Thanks." His words were soft and his face embarrassed. "I need to hit the head." Ben nodded toward the men's room as a petite lady her age appeared.

Rayna doubted Ben needed to pee that urgently; it was his pride that sent him through the faded door.

Good, gives me a chance to get a room with a single bed and convince him it was the only one available.

"Hi, I'd like a room, please."

The lady smiled. "Sure, I'm Megan. Just fill out the registry, and I'll get you all set."

While she filled out the form, a man appeared behind the lady—a very attractive man. "You called?"

"Oh, geez, Sam, stop sneaking up on me like that. You scared the shit out of me. I didn't call for you." The woman spoke as if she were playing, and when Rayna saw the look in her soft brown eyes when she stared up at the man, she witnessed pure, unadulterated love. It caused a zing of longing to shoot through her heart.

"You didn't call for me yet, but you were just about to. I saved you the trouble." Same dropped a kiss on her head and then took notice of Rayna. He seemed to study her and sum her up instantly, giving an almost imperceptible nod that made her think he approved.

"Was that your husband, Mrs...." Megan looked at the line she'd just filled out. "Wilson?"

"No, he's my boyfriend. I mean my ex-boyfriend, but I wanted to talk to you about that. I know you don't know me from Adam, but my car broke down, and we don't have a lot of money, and well, I love him, and I was hoping you could..." Rayna's words died on her lips as she noticed Ben emerge from the restroom. She had no idea what possessed her to spill her secrets to this stranger, but she had been going all-in. Now, she had doubts about her tactics. "Never mind."

Ben stepped up next to her. "I hope they had a few available rooms or at least a double?"

Rayna was crushed under the weight of his words. Her chance had just evaporated at a roadside inn in Nevada. Even so, she let her eyes make a plea to the stranger, hoping Megan understood enough.

Her bubbly words and generous offer told Rayna she'd missed it. "Sure, I've got a double and a king that have been updated so both have oversized tubs, and microwaves. I could cut you a deal on them since you're stuck and all." Megan took a big dump on what little hope she had that fate might be her ally.

Rayna felt her face fall at the same time Ben breathed a relieved sigh by her side.

"That's great." Rayna's words said she was thrilled with the room arrangement, while her heart felt anything but.

Sam appeared back by Megan's side, and this time, he studied both her and Ben. It was almost unsettling until he smirked. "Sorry, babe, those are out of commission, *remember*." The last was said with an upward inflection like a question, and the couple exchanged a look Rayna couldn't quite identify. "The only room we have available is the old honeymoon suite."

He turned his dark piercing gaze to Rayna. "Sorry about that, but we're doing renovations, and well, it's not a bad room. A little outdated but cozy. I can see if I can find and dust off a rollaway for you. It might not fit well in there, but you're welcome to try. Sorry, Miss Wilson, I know you'd asked for two rooms."

Rayna cut her eyes toward Ben. *Was he buying this?* Because she sure wasn't.

"Oh, that's right, dear. Sorry, guys, I totally spaced."

Apparently, Ben was the only one who hadn't caught on. Megan was grinning like she'd just rescued a basket of impossibly adorable kittens, and Sam winked with a grin of his own.

Luckily, Ben had bent to grab their bags and missed the worst performance she'd witnessed since she watched the recording of her Eliza Doolittle in fourth grade.

"Here's your key, folks. If you need anything at all, just ask us. Hope you enjoy your stay."

Rayna mouthed "thank you," before taking the plastic fob and following Ben toward their room. She glanced back before the door closed and saw Sam and Megan embrace each other while watching them head toward the "only" available room.

Plastic key fob, hand-written register, and owners who involved themselves with their guests? This place was old school-old school. Rayne didn't know these places existed, but here they were.

It wasn't the best plan she'd ever had. Hell, it might have been her worst, but she had to go all-in. They were heading toward Vegas, after all.

CHAPTER 2

Fuck, fuck, fuck.

It was the only word marching through Ben's head as they walked toward their room. *This is not good, not good at all. Alone with Ray overnight, in a honeymoon suite, nonetheless.*

This arrangement had been a bad idea from the beginning. Ben knew spending time with her would only sharpen the feelings he'd been working overtime to dull over the last months.

The love he'd buried was like a damned zombie, and the minute she smiled at him, that undead bastard clawed its way out of the grave he'd hidden it in.

The only thing protecting him from the bite that would transform him back into *her man* was remembering her accusations and lack of trust.

No matter how much he begged her to trust him, she wouldn't, or couldn't. Either way, the venom and disgust she spewed at him had finally ended their relationship. He'd been willing to stay after all that, if she could've only trusted him in the future and let the past go.

Sure, they would've had a better shot if she'd believed him to start with, but she hadn't, and he had even been willing to settle if it meant moving forward.

Ben was ready for marriage and kids and a mortgage—the whole nine-yards. And he wanted it with her, always with her.

Looking over at her profile, he remembered all the reasons why. Rayna was a good person, with a gentle soul, a perfect ass, and a heart-stopping smile.

Her golden hair mesmerized him when it caught in the breeze and her green eyes held him prisoner. If only she…they…hadn't let Treena close enough to poison them, they could've weathered the storm. The storm he hadn't caused but was guilty of all the same.

Benton was slightly shocked when they opened the door. It was like a trip back in time, and the term suite was a drastic over-sale. Shag carpet, heart-shaped bed, and a loveseat that looked to be crushed velvet.

If the situation weren't so fucked-up, he'd have laughed at the sight. Just as Sam had said, there was no room for a roll-away, and the truth of that statement was staring back at him through the open door.

No way his six-foot frame could fit on that love seat, and he wasn't such an asshole that he would ask Ray to sleep there. There wasn't a damn thing he could do at this point, and he was fucked. Sharing a heart-shaped bed with the woman he would always love was going to be torture. The only thing left to do was pray Bubba, or whatever his name was, got the car fixed in record time and they could continue as planned, sooner rather than later.

Not exactly as planned. He wasn't going to hold Ray to her end of the bargain. He needed to cut his losses and protect his heart. He'd find another way to prove to his potential client that he was a family man, settled and good at his word. If he were to be honest with himself, he didn't really need Ray for that. He could've asked anyone, but deep down, he'd wanted to spend time with her, and it had been the perfect excuse.

Once they broke the threshold and fully entered the room, Ben felt a sense of dread and peace wash over him. As he turned to observe his surroundings, he caught Ray's shy, apologetic smile. He still loved everything about her, well, almost everything. Being here with her in a run-down honeymoon suite felt…natural.

They'd planned it all out by the freshman year of college. Junior year, they would drive to Vegas, get hitched by Elvis, stay in a roadside room just like this to celebrate, and then keep it as their private secret until after they each graduated and were established in their careers. Then they would have a wedding for everyone else.

Ben mourned the loss of that dream. If they had stuck to the plan, they would've been married months before his world went sideways and their relationship went south.

Maybe if we had stuck to our plan, Ray would've felt more secure and not assumed the worst of me. Maybe if I hadn't kept putting it off, it wouldn't…what's the point. What's done is done. Now, I just need to get through this. Then we can both go our separate ways, and I can keep on being miserable.

A part of him didn't want them taking two different paths. A part, actually all of him, wanted the path they had laid out to be theirs…together. But Ray's lack of trust in him cut deep. She took her best friend's word over his, and then, rather than make a clean break, she turned into a nightmare girlfriend.

Granted, it had been his idea for her to just try to forget it rather than continue to push for her to believe him, but that didn't explain how cruel she was at every turn. It emasculated him to the point they weren't even having sex the last few weeks. Of course, she thought it was because he was sleeping around and couldn't stomach the thought of her not being a twig with fake tits.

Looking back, Ben knew Treena was the root of all that insecurity. Ray was a confident girl before she'd met Treena, but Treena preyed on Ray. That witch kept her down on herself so she could feel more secure. Ben tried to gently point it out once, and it had blown up in his face. Ray was fiercely loyal; it was one of the things he loved about her. *But why did her loyalty not extend to me then?*

That was a question that had plagued him ever since their break-up.

"So, I'll go back to the office and grab some extra linens, and we can rock, paper, scissors for the loveseat?"

It had to be a joke since neither of them could fit on that damned thing.

"Real funny, Ray. You may be petite, but you'd have to be downright elf height to have a chance at fitting."

Ben turned in time to see her drop her bag and then plop down on the furniture in question, nearly taking up the whole thing just to sit back. Loveseat may have been an overestimation; large chair was a more apt description.

"Whoa, no one has called me petite since sixth grade." Her words said humor, but her voice said hurt. She really did believe she was fat, and Ben hated it.

Ray wasn't a twig, but she wasn't Mama June sized either. She had curves, beautiful curves in all the right places, but she was not fat. Maybe next to some anorexic model types, she would appear large, but she was anything but.

That was the standard she strived for after meeting Treena. Always jumping from diet to diet, but nothing made her a size two, and Ben liked her just the way she was. She'd drunk vinegar and eaten kale for damn near three weeks before she broke down after having only dropped two pounds. His Ray was meant to look like a woman, not a twig.

"Ray, you know better. You are perfect just the way you are. Stop letting other people slap a label on you."

"If I'm so perfect, then why wasn't I enough for you?" The words were low, barely audible, but Ben heard them. A sad sigh preceded and followed her words.

Ben dropped everything he had been carrying, both emotionally and physically, if just for a moment, and approached her.

Ray's beautiful green eyes went wide with shock and maybe a little suspicion. Sinking to his knees, Ben took her face in his hands. He was wholly unprepared for the contact and what it did to him, and if her face was relaying information correctly, so was she. Her eyes slid closed, and she tipped her face to nuzzle into his touch.

He only wanted to tell her she was always enough, instead, his lips descended until they met hers. It was like no time had passed but also a lifetime. Passion wasn't ruling his actions; it was connection and comfort. He needed her to feel enough.

Regretfully, he pulled back. "You were always enough, Ray. Always."

The protest was poised on her flushed pink lips still damp from his kiss. He let his thumb slide over them to silence her words while he took note of something which had always fascinated him, the juxtaposition of *them*.

His dark brown against her creamy, slightly peach-tinted skin. It was a picture of pure beauty and boundaries broken. Ben had spent many waking hours just gliding his hands up and down her sleeping form relishing their differences.

In that moment, however, if he didn't stop, he would be making love to her and planning how many kids they were going to have. He wanted that more than anything, but their relationship could never succeed without trust, and he didn't know how to earn hers back while forgiving her for being hateful.

"Ray, you are enough, in all aspects, now…I'm starving, and I saw they had a little diner. What do you say we grab a bite, then come back here and play Netflix roulette? Save everything else for tomorrow? Deal?"

At her nod, Ben dropped his hands and helped her stand. They headed for the door. "But—"

Ben spun around. "Wow, I'm proud of you. You held out a whole three seconds before you started overthinking things. I said we'll worry about *everything* later; the only thing that even has to be addressed tonight is sleeping arrangements, and well, that's not really a concern since there is only one possible answer. We're both adults and can share a bed without problems."

Sure, that sounded real confident. He knew there would be issues, but he wanted her at ease. She didn't need to know he'd lie awake all night sweating and probably have to bang one out in the shower just to survive. Ray had enough worry without adding that. He would be a perfect gentleman.

"Okay."

The diner was small, but the smells coming from it were amazing, and he was certainly starving. Luckily, he had enough cash to at least buy her dinner here so he didn't feel like a complete loser.

After they were seated and placed their order, the silence was awkward, at best. It was like Ray had something to say but refused to. She kept her purse on her lap and kept staring into it like it held answers.

This was not what Ben wanted. He had started seeing this forced togetherness as a chance. A chance to clear the air, maybe a chance to have his best friend back…possibly even a second chance at the plans they'd had.

Ben stared into her soft features. Her pouty lips and rounded cheeks were captivating. If only she'd shift her eyes to his so he could catch a glimpse into her soul. Ray's eyes always gave her away, but she wouldn't look up from her damn bag.

"Earth to Rayna. Your burger is getting cold. What's so interesting in there, anyway?" Ben made to lean over the table as she snapped her purse closed.

"Nothing. I was…just lost in thought."

Ben wanted to question her further. It was clear that wasn't the whole story, but Ray took a bite of her burger and moaned. All other thoughts escaped him. She enjoyed her food. She didn't order a salad and push carrots around her plate. No, Ray wasn't afraid to eat and show her appreciation for a good burger. It was just one of the many things he loved about her.

Her sounds brought other thoughts to mind, and he adjusted himself before his zipper left a permanent scar on his dick. When her tongue darted out to capture a bit of juice that dripped from her lips, he actually groaned. Clearing his throat to cover up his unexpected sound, he tried to make a joke. "Sounds like a good burger."

"Oh, my God, it is," she answered between sucking her fingers.

Fuck, how can I make it through a few days when I can't even make it through one meal without picturing her lips wrapped around my cock until her cheeks hollow?

Ray's eyes lifted to his, and he glimpsed the past, present, and future. The ghosts that haunted her seemed to have fled momentarily. She was looking at him like he was just Ben—not Ben the unfaithful—and she was the woman who loved him. A trace of a smile lifted her lips, and Ben wondered if she could read his thoughts as her tongue darted out once more, this time not searching for anything in particular.

Her lip followed her tongue back into the dark cavern of her mouth, and she worried it with her perfect white teeth. Ben recognized that look, and it sent his libido into overdrive.

That was all the encouragement he needed, that they could be Ray and Ben again, R & B. It didn't matter what happened in the past; they could start over now. It was all right there in her jade depths. Ben was sure he could make her forget the past, and Lord knew he could if it meant having a future with her.

He was ready to let go of everything and even apologize if that's what it took for her to be his. That's what she'd wanted back then. Just an apology and she was willing to let things go. He'd been too stubborn to give it. He'd wanted her to see the truth, but the truth didn't matter if it meant never seeing that look again.

The only question in his mind was if she wanted the same, and by the way she was squirming on the red vinyl, he was sure the answer was yes. At least, she wanted him physically, and that was as good a place as any to start.

"Dessert?" Ben tilted his head to the old-fashioned pie case sitting on the counter. "I don't know about you, but that cherry pie looks like it should come with a warning label, and I am not about to pass that up."

CHAPTER 3

Ben had been right, but then again, he had an eye for those things. Picking the best dessert, no matter where they were was his superpower. Even when Ray didn't know what she wanted and would be torn between two sugary confections, Ben would just know.

Somehow, he always ordered the perfect finish to every meal. And just like old times, he ate his slower so she could steal a few bites after she'd polished hers off.

Ben was being so…Ben, she felt guilty for the room deception. He deserved better than being tricked into giving them another chance. First thing in the morning, she'd ask for another room and just split it on her four almost maxed out credit cards.

The short walk back to the room was pleasant except for the guilt gnawing at her gut. Ben fell right back into the role of doting boyfriend-ish. That just increased the speed of the razor-sharp teeth chomping away at her.

When Ben opened the door and ushered her in, his hand lingered on her lower back, singeing her skin. Ray excused herself to change into her comfy pajamas as Ben grabbed the remote and plopped down on the chair-sized sofa.

"Ray, pick a letter and a number." His voice carried into the bathroom. A ghost of a smile graced her lips, but it held more than a hint of sadness. Netflix roulette was their thing. She studied her reflection a bit longer. She was a bitch. Tricking a good man into spending time with her…*who does that?*

"Tomorrow, I'll fix this." Looking deep into her own eyes in the reflection, she realized the past she'd been clinging to shouldn't really matter anymore. As much as she'd told herself…and him…she needed his confession and apology for closure, she really didn't. Not anymore. Maybe not ever. She'd just been so devastated. Once Treena sent her that horrible picture, it was seared into her mind.

She let her gaze travel the length of her body in the mirror. Yep, she was larger, but she'd never been uncomfortable with that before, not until Treena told her that was why Ben had strayed. However, he didn't seem to be turned off by her. Maybe she let his one indiscretion and Treena get into her head.

Either way, she was done letting it drive her, affect her...affect Ben. She'd done enough damage, and it was over now. When she saw Ben's face for the first time since they broke up, the pain she'd caused was glaring back at her. But even with all that, he seemed willing to put it behind them and be friends. If he could do it, she could, too.

They'd both made mistakes, and it was time to adult and move on.

"D three." Having given him the Netflix roulette number, she took a deep breath and exited the bathroom.

"Looks like Deadpool, Ray." She dropped onto the couch next to him and practically landed on his lap. As he shifted his body, she felt the weight of his gaze. Ben was eating her up with his eyes. When his line of sight shifted down her legs, a grin split his face.

"Wow, Ray. You look...hell, I can't believe these haven't fallen apart yet." She shivered under his touch as he ran his hand over the worn-thin flannel material. Ray noted after a few passes, Ben let his hand take up residence on her thigh.

"Yep, and knock on wood" —Ray rapped on his head gently— "they've got another couple of decades in them." Ray propped her head on the hand. The one that had damn near moved from his head to around his neck. She allowed herself to lean into him just a little and brought her other foot up under her ample ass.

Ben squeezed her knee gently and guided her head down to his shoulder with his free hand. Ray didn't read too much into it. Ben liked to snuggle when watching TV; he just did.

Ray heard something about a long night and her pajamas, but she was half-asleep. She allowed herself the comfort of being tucked into Ben for one last time and relished it.

"Wha—" The sensation of floating brought her halfway into consciousness; she must've dozed off.

"Shush, just sleep." Ben's voice cut through the fog as he carried her to the bed and gently deposited her before shucking his shirt and tucking his body around hers. Having his hard physique pressed into her brought her further to awareness.

"Ben, I can sleep—" Ray tried to get up, but Ben held her tighter, pulling her back into the little spoon position while burrowing his face into the back of her neck. *It feels so good. God, it feels golden.*

"Just let me hold you, Ray. We're adults, and I will be a perfect gentleman. Just grant me this one concession?"

As she relaxed into him again, she pondered so many things. She didn't want to hurt him anymore. She was honestly going to fix this tomorrow. But for tonight, she'd let him have his way with the sleeping arrangement and she'd let herself fall into the dream of them until the harsh morning light melted it away.

Allowing herself one stolen indulgence, she covered the arm that was wrapped around her belly with her own and let her fingertips drift back and forth until sleep started pulling her under. She heard Ben groan, which wasn't unexpected—this was another of those couple things he'd always enjoyed.

While Ray wasn't a super cuddly person, Ben more than made up for the both of them. It didn't matter what they were doing or where they were, he'd always have to be touching her in some fashion. If he entered a room where she was, he went out of his way for anything from a small caress to a full-on ass grab.

She'd never really appreciated that part of his nature until they were broken up and she realized how deeply she missed those little moments they shared. The ones that seemed unimportant at the time. Actions she'd taken for granted.

Visions of Ben, the Ben she dreamt about every night, drifted in and out of her head along with his voice.

The dreams had seemed to get more vivid as time marched on. Especially tonight, even with the real thing right there. "I miss this so fucking much, love you, Ray." Dream Ben's voice was so real, it felt as if he'd actually said it.

"Same. Always the same," she groggily whispered into the night and waited. Waited for the vision that would burst the bubble and pull her out of her drift into dreamland.

For the most part, it was always the same. Dream Ben would be saying or doing the absolute perfect thing and they'd be happy, really happy, then, the next thing she knew, he'd be pumping away into Treena. She'd turn into a harpy and scream and wail, then the dream would be destroyed.

Ray would get up, splash her face, and lie awake for hours until exhaustion pulled her under without dreams, without visions, and without Ben.

She bolted up in bed. A cursory glance in all directions told her she was in the hotel and Ben was sound asleep and slightly snoring beside her. What pulled her from her sleep wasn't the vision that had haunted her every sleeping and waking hour for damn near a year, it was the lack of it.

Ben slept in a similar pose, just without the skank draped on him, and no twinge of pain attacked her. No feeling of inadequacy assaulted her—nothing. Well, not exactly *nothing*. She was turned on like crazy.

That shocked her, because as much as she'd still wanted him after everything that happened, she couldn't look at him without a wave of pain washing away any other feelings.

"I am throwing that picture away tomorrow and getting you your own room. You deserve at least that," she mumbled her promise to the quiet darkness. No longer needing to torture herself with the visual reminder was freeing.

I forgive you, Ray.

Silently, she laughed at the absurdity that it took a broken drive shaft and an outdated honeymoon suite for her to forgive herself and let everything go. Letting go didn't just mean the pain inducing bits and pieces, but the hope of being R & B again. She released it all and set them both free.

It hadn't occurred to her before how she was holding them both hostage to the past, but she was. She was definitely getting him his own room if possible and confessing how she steered their room situation to her advantage. Ben was a good man and didn't deserve someone who was manipulative and unforgiving.

He deserves so much better.

And she most certainly didn't deserve him.

She relaxed back into her pillow and turned to face Ben. His features were soft in repose. No tension, no past, no worries. His slight snoring sounded more like purring, which she'd always found sexy as hell. Allowing one finger to lightly trace his masculine jawline caused a shudder to course through her body.

He repositioned himself, and Ray jerked her hand back, not wanting to get caught molesting the man in his sleep. Ben reached for her and folded her into his embrace, trapping her against his chest.

Tomorrow was a new day with a new room hopefully, but tonight, she would lie in his arms and pretend. Her hand tentatively found its way around his toned abs as her knee drifted north. Ben sighed in his sleep, holding her tighter before loosening his hold and letting his strong arm drop on top of hers.

"I forgive you, Ben. I forgive us both." Her words were barely a whisper as she spoke them into the dated hotel room, but they were a scream of release to her soul.

Her grumbling stomach demanded food. When she woke, the first thing she saw was wood paneling. Where the hell was she that had wood paneling? And whose warm body was next to her? Before she panicked and leaped from the bed, the memory of the last twenty-four hours seeped back into her sleep-clouded mind. Benton, the busted drive shaft, her deception. Her stomach interrupted her mental inventory.

A few of those things were out of her control, but not everything. She could fix the hunger and try to make up for the deception.

She popped out of bed and headed for the bathroom. Once she did the bare minimum to make herself slightly human, she snagged her wallet and snuck out of the room, leaving Ben snoozing away.

The diner was her first stop to order biscuits and gravy, with hash browns—Ben's favorite. She took the fifteen-minute prep time to head to the office and talk to Sam or Megan, whichever one happened to be there, and straighten out this whole mess.

Megan spotted her first. "Rayna, to what do we owe the pleasure? Everything all right with the room, I hope?" Sam turned at the sound of Megan's voice.

Great, I get to face them both in my shame.

"Yes, everything is fine...as it can be anyway. I...um, want to apologize for what I asked of you, or kind of asked of you. I should never have tried to trick Ben, and I damn sure should've never asked you to participate in my deception." She paused to take a much-needed deep breath.

Once composed, she tried again. "I appreciate how you" —she turned her attention to Sam— "picked up on my secret plea, but it was wrong of me, and I would like to add another room. I'll have to spread it across a few cards, but—"

"Sorry, dear, there are no other rooms available."

"But you said" —she turned toward Sam— "then you said." Why were they not getting this was what she really wanted? Were they still trying to hook her up?

"Sam was right; he always is. I just forgot. You know how it is, scatterbrained sometimes. Anyway, see, no deception, so no harm, no foul." A look passed between the couple, but Ray's head was spinning too fast to try to decipher it. "Is there anything else you need?"

"Um, no, wait…yes, can I have an extra blanket?"

"You need more than the spare in the closet? Sure, we can have Shelly bring over a few."

"I'm such an idiot. I never even checked. No, that's fine. Thanks, but if a room becomes available, will you please let me know?"

"Sure thing, enjoy your stay. Oh, have you heard from Bud?"

Ray almost forgot about the car. "Not yet, but I wasn't expecting to with the holiday. I hope it's soon." *For the sake of doing the right thing*, she added mentally.

"It will be. He called this morning looking for you, said he must've written your number down wrong, so I gave him your room number. I hope that's okay. I figured you'd want any news as soon as possible so you two can get on to wherever you were headed."

Megan was really sweet, and Ray could see them being good friends if she hadn't met her by trying to enlist her help in seducing her ex.

"That's perfect. I really appreciate it, and yes, sooner is better. Thanks."

With a wave, Ray headed back to the diner to pick up white Styrofoam containers that would make Ben's morning.

The short walk back to the room gave her a touch of nostalgia. She was walking slow and remembering the third anniversary of their first official date.

Ray had enlisted the help of her friend, Rachel, who worked in the dining hall. Together, they whipped up a homemade southern breakfast—biscuits and gravy, complete with grits and hash browns.

Yep, a carb-loaded southern mama's dream, but they were Ben's favorite, and she had wanted to do something special for him since he only got that kind of treat when he went home on winter break. A laugh bubbled up from her chest. "Makes perfect sense for someone born and bred in New Mexico."

Ben had never even been to the south, hell, neither had she, but his mother was deep south through and through, and it sort of became *their thing*. The laughter turned to a sexy smile when what happened when she entered his dorm room that day came rushing back.

Ben had taken one whiff of the contents as she placed the containers on the desk and sat down next to them.

Her breath turned heavy as the memory became downright tactile.

The way he'd cupped her cheeks was gentle, but the look in his eyes, feral. That look promised naughty things that he most certainly delivered on that day. He'd licked his lips, catching his full lower one between his pearly white teeth.

Ben knew that look drove her insane. He'd pinned her with his chocolate gaze as he lowered his lips to hers excruciatingly slow. When they finally met, the zap of sexual energy hitched her breath.

His tongue invaded her mouth, conquering her heart for good. Swallowing each other's moans had been an out-of-body experience that ended abruptly as he'd dropped to his knees, slid her underwear to the side with little finesse, and proceeded to enjoy a pre-breakfast appetizer.

While his approach had been clumsy, his technique was anything but. Benton was a man possessed, and that time had been totally different. Before then, they'd always been…methodical. They were each other's firsts and had learned together, so it was always in a bed. Always good, but never outside of the box.

That had been the first time he called her Cookie. After he used his tongue to bring her to a knee-weakening orgasm. Then, he ripped her panties off and lifted her fat ass as if she weighed nothing and slammed his cock into her like he never had before. He'd fucked her up against his dorm wall as his trophies and lightsabers dropped to the ground.

Still, he kept going, not caring about his accolades or collectable He'd only cared about pleasing her.

Her body caught fire just thinking about it. That day had changed everything. Their sex life had never been better, and it opened them both up to exploration.

Not to mention as they laid in bed afterward, the breakfast all eaten, Ben asked her to marry him and pulled the most amazing ring out from under her pillow.

The last thought had her shaking off the memory. That part was too painful to remember because she wanted that ring back, that day back, that Ben back.

Ray balanced the Styrofoam in one hand as she fished the key from her pocket, again noting the empty finger that taunted her as she turned the lock.

"Ray!" Ben practically shouted as he rested the phone receiver in its cradle. He leaped off the bed to help, took the food with an appreciative whiff, and deposited it on the end table. "Um, that was…" Ben indicated to the phone and rubbed the back of his neck, the way he did when he was uncomfortable. God, she'd made him uncomfortable. That wasn't her intention; she'd just wanted to make him happy.

It wasn't until she was on her way back to the room that the memory attached to the breakfast had come.

"That was, um…me calling for extra blankets since I'm sharing the bed with an Olympic gold medalist in cover hogging." His laugh was rich and soothing and made her feel things in her lady bits she had no business feeling.

Not anymore.

CHAPTER 4

"Gold in both summer and winter, thank you very much." The snarky bow accompanied by her blinding smile made Ben want to toss her on the bed and make love to her until she agreed to drive to Vegas and get hitched. "But, I already checked with the office about getting extra blankets, and…"

She sashayed to the closet neither had bothered to open until now, flung open the narrow door, and reached inside.

"Viola." When she turned, she had a plastic-wrapped bundle of sheets and blankets, which she promptly chucked at him with a laugh.

Instead of catching the projectile, he batted it away and rushed her. "Oh, is that how we're going to play?" Ben lifted her up, and she must've read the intentions in his eyes. *She always could.*

"Don't you dare. I mean it." Her voice rose as he made his way to the bed holding her high. "Benton James Davis! You better not be thinking what I think you are."

He answered her with a wink as they floated down to the bed. "Ben, noooooo—" Her words were cut off as he proceeded to tickle her senseless.

"Ben…staaaaappp." Those were the only choppy words he heard between her bouts of laughter. Ben raised her shirt and raspberried her stomach, then nuzzled it affectionately.

Her skin still smelled the same—sweet like the sugar cookie body butter she apparently still used.

It wasn't the first time he'd done such a playful thing. Hell, at the height of their relationship, this had been a damn near daily occurrence. And it almost always led to naked fun time. *I'd give anything for naked fun time right about now.*

Ben was so lost in the past possibly being their future, he hadn't noticed that everything in the room ceased. Her laughter, her breathing, hell, even the dust motes in the air seemed to have stopped and hovered above them.

He was too far down the rabbit hole already, and Ben acted on what his heart and body wanted. Instead of levering up and offering an apology like a gentleman should've, he took a different approach. A step in the exact opposite direction of gentlemanly.

Sliding up her body in a track that made his cock even harder, he dragged his nose through the vee of her top and along the side of her neck.

"God, you smell good enough to eat, Ray." The words slipped from his mouth in a spontaneous confession the moment before his lips tracked their way to hers.

Their matching groans harmonized in the most beautiful song. Ray's lips parted, and he took full advantage, slipping his tongue into a velvet heaven he knew so well and missed so terribly.

It was like a homecoming, a return to the terra firma some unseen force tethered him to no matter how long he'd been away. But as her hips rose to grind against his granite-hard cock, reality seeped into his consciousness.

Ray had brought him their breakfast and how was she rewarded?

With a lie and sexual advances.

A lie he hadn't intended to tell but did all the same. An advance his very soul wanted but was wrong under the circumstances.

Maybe if he hadn't lied about Bud calling saying how by some miracle he had the part lying around and the car was ready, he could've let their enjoyment of each other continue.

Perhaps if he hadn't told Bud they couldn't take delivery of her car until tomorrow, he could've sunk his cock into her welcoming body until she agreed to forgive him and promised to stay. It didn't matter one damn bit that he hadn't cheated; he'd confess and apologize if it meant her pain would go away, but she never would.

Guilt pulled him from the bed and the cradle of her hips. He extended his hand to aid her up. "Ray, I'm sorry. I don't know what came over me. Actually, I do know, but I'm sorry all the same. You brought me breakfast and took care of all this and even agreed to help me out and I attack you like so—"

"No, Ben." She smoothed her clothes and spoke to her feet. "Don't apologize for that, never for that. It's just…I. I mean…" Ray trailed off as if the words she wanted didn't exist. He hated seeing her uncomfortable.

"You don't have to explain, love. I get it, and if you want the truth…" He leaned in close, taking in another lungful of her. Would he ever get enough? "I'm not sorry at all."

Before he could confess more, he left her personal space, snatched the top divided container from the table along with a fork and napkin kit, and spun to land on the bed.

"Besides, I smell heaven in here, and I'm starving." He opened the lid and took a whiff to really sell the idea he was only talking about the food. While he did feel horrible about lying to her, he didn't feel as bad as he should.

After a few orgasmic bites, Ben cleared his mouth long enough to speak. "Oh, Ray, you always did know the way to my heart. Do you know how long it's been since I last had biscuits and gravy?"

Ray had tucked into hers beside him on the bed with her legs crossed and a huge gravy spot on her shirt. A tiny drop sat at the corner of her mouth when her chewing stopped, and she looked at him like a deer caught in headlights.

Unable to resist, he swiped the white gold with his thumb and sucked it into his mouth. Never taking his eyes of hers, he didn't miss the spark of arousal that danced across her perfect green irises. He fucking wanted her more than he ever had. His dilemma was how best to go about it.

As for wanting to fuck him, that wasn't an issue, never really had been except toward the last few weeks of their relationship. The problems facing him were harder than just getting her turned on. Rayna Beth Wilson was not one of those women from the books she liked to secretly read who could be manipulated and led around by her pussy. No, no matter how good he gave it to her, she would follow her heart instead of the place in her pants where his brain currently resided.

He had to find a way around his little deception about the car. That also seemed doable. A little finesse would be required, but not out of the realm of possibility.

The one that gave him the most concern was the past. Would she be able to forgive him for an infidelity he wasn't sure he could cop to? He wasn't guilty, but he had been a hair's breadth from confessing anyway last night as he drifted off with her in his arms.

If she had seemed to be in the same mental space as she had been the night before when she entered the door weighted down with breakfast, he might have done just that.

But something was different today.

She was different.

A certain amount of something he couldn't identify had settled around her. It almost felt like acceptance or forgiveness or maybe she'd simply and finally let go.

He had, too. Spending this time with her, no matter how brief, brought a whole new perspective to what they'd gone through when they'd been careening toward a break-up.

For so long, Ben had held on to the *raging bitch* behavior she'd exhibited, to keep his pain at bay. It had started as small accusations. She would ask him how she looked in an outfit and nothing he could say would make her happy. *Maybe if I looked like Treena, you'd think I was beautiful,* she'd snap. It was little things like that, months before she'd even accused him of cheating. It was like she wanted to make him suffer or something. That was the harbinger of the end.

Ray had stopped initiating sex altogether. In hindsight, he should've done something, but at the time, he couldn't see how badly Treena was tearing her down. It was crystal fucking clear later, but back then, not so much.

Instead of trying to help her, Ben took every shitty word she'd flung at him and tucked it away. The death knell came when his shoulder had finally healed enough for him to start a more intensive, sport-specific rehab.

It had quickly become obvious to Ben that he'd never be a starter again, hell, he wasn't even second or third string. He was destined for coaching or player management, at best. Even with the rough patch they'd been going through, he knew the only comfort for his broken soul and shattered dreams was Ray.

Ben needed her more than he'd ever needed another living being that day, and instead of the loving arms and healing love-making he expected, he'd walked into the icing on the cake of the worst fucking day of his life.

"Babe, we need to talk, but can we please do it naked? I need…" When he'd stepped in the room and looked up, there she'd been, crying and shaking.

The rest came flooding back, but Ben willed himself to stay in the present. Ray moaning over breakfast helped.

He missed those sounds. God, how he fucking missed those sounds. More than that, he missed causing them.

All he could do was stare at her over the plastic fork full of biscuit he'd halted halfway to his mouth. Her eyes were closed as she chewed, and the sounds just kept falling from her lips.

Ben abandoned his breakfast on the opposite side table and just watched her eat. It was more sensual than it should have been. When her tongue dashed out to lick the last of the gravy from her fork, he couldn't hold back his own groan of pleasure.

Tongue paused in mid-air, her eyes turned toward him, and he had to adjust his cock. Just that slight touch caused a hiss to escape him. Thank God he was still in pajamas instead of his day clothes or the circulation to his manly assets would have been cut off.

The desire to lean forward and suck her pretty pink tongue into his mouth was damn near overwhelming. Sadly, it retreated back into her mouth. She uncrossed her legs, leaned forward and she dropped her empty container to the worn wood surface. Ben continued to stare as she re-crossed her legs while wiping her hands on a napkin.

"What? It was good. Can't a girl appreciate a good biscuit without judgment?" While she'd said words that used to trigger an argument over how fat she thought she was, her face was alight with humor instead of self-doubt and insecurities.

"There's nothing sexier than a woman who knows a good white gravy when she tastes one." Ben watched her eyes drop to her lap, and she worried the frayed napkin that she'd all but destroyed. "Hey now, you know I'm not judging. Ray, even with all the bullshit, you have to know, your weight was never an issue for me, right? I love it when you eat, and…" He allowed one hand to land on her knee. "You know how much I love those fucking curves."

Could he have misread so much? She seemed so self-confident now, loving herself, but maybe…

Her eyes met his once more, and the answer was there. He hadn't. "Oh, God, no Ben, it's not that at all." His eyes dove to her knee where his hand rested as hers landed on top of his. "It's just. I need—"

He raised his gaze back to hers and saw desire. There was something bothering her, but it was being suppressed by raw sexual need. *Maybe this once, her pussy can lead her…right back to me.*

Benton lunged forward and claimed her lips. So much pent-up passion was trapped in him, ready to explode out, that his teeth slammed into hers. Her mouth met his with equal passion, and he was lost. *None of the old bullshit matters; what matters is right here and now.*

He pulled his mouth from hers and kissed and tasted his way across her cheek and down her neck. When he gave her a playful bite, her hands found their way to his head and held him there. He got the message loud and clear.

Ben nibbled his way to her ear, kissing and licking and sucking. "Oh, God, Ben. Yes." No words had ever sounded sweeter. He tracked one hand down her front and then back up again, but under her shirt, enjoying the slide of his palm against her creamy skin.

With the flick of a finger, he unsnapped her bra, then hesitated. They were about to pass that point of no return. Benton knew once he held that perfect globe in his hand, pinching and plumping the nipple…once he had it in his mouth, neither would stop until they were spent.

With a reverence he should've always touched her with, he ghosted his fingers teasingly across her nipple, not lingering. The moan it drew from her lips was earth shattering

Returning his mouth to hers, he hovered above it, searching her eyes—for what, he didn't know. "Make love to me, Ray?"

Her mouth spoke with action while her eyes spoke with silent words. They screamed *yes* as her lips lifted to his, searing and flawless.

"All the yes I need, baby girl." Her lips muffled his words while he thumbed her nipple to attention. He couldn't wait to taste her again. Ending the kiss, he slid slightly down her body. He pushed her shirt up and finally took her breast into his mouth. He feasted on one and then the other while shoving her shirt higher and higher until she aided him in being rid of it altogether.

"Oh, God." The invocation that fell from her lips fanned the flames even higher. While still tasting her perky pink nipples, he rid her of her leggings, and there she was. He gave a soft bite before he released her breast with a wet pop.

"You're fucking perfect, always have been." Ben stood and removed his own clothes and got on his knees between her calves. He let his hands roam up and down her legs, digging his fingers in her soft flesh. His eyes followed his hands as one didn't return down to her knee.

Instead, he parted her glistening lips with his fingers, again fascinated by the juxtaposition of them. As one finger sank into her heat, he had to bite his lip to keep from practically fucking coming on the bedspread. "Oh, for fuck's sake, Ben, you know what that does to me." Her words drew his attention.

Her focus was obviously divided between his lip disappearing behind his teeth and his finger disappearing into her. But he knew she referred to his lip. It was a confession she'd made to him after the first time they'd slept together.

Ben couldn't count the number of times he'd used it to get her in the mood quickly when they were cramming for finals or he was upping his training for a big game.

Now, it was different, though. He was relishing the looks she was giving him. Taking mental snapshots in case it was the last time. He shook off that thought before it softened his cock and turned his attention to his finger, advancing and retreating.

"Um, you look good enough to eat, and I am craving my sugar cookie." Her laughter didn't slow him down one bit as he fell into her pussy face-first.

One swipe of his tongue told him that while everything had changed, nothing had. Her taste, her feel, her…it was definitely a homecoming.

CHAPTER 5

Ray covered her face in embarrassment. She remembered him calling her his sugar cookie, but he'd never said it while he was actually looking at her vajayjay. Ben had joked before or after but never during. "Oh, my God, Ben. Cut it…ahhh."

Ahhh was the sound words made when they died. Hers met their end swiftly with one flick of his tongue.

Scorching was the temperature of his mouth and maddening was the pace of his fingers. She tried to suck in oxygen only to find her lungs on vacation. When his lava-like tongue circled her clit and his teeth gently raked it, her lungs returned as she gulped air. "Fuuuuuck."

It was all there was to say, a long drawn out, intake F-bomb; it summed up the moment adequately.

It had been a year since any man, really only Benton, had touched her in that way, and oh, what a way it was.

The same, yet different.

Ben had always been good in the bedroom, but somehow, he'd gotten even better.

Her hands gripped his head, and she dug her nails into the flesh. Ben wasn't bald, but he didn't have enough hair to really get a grip so a girl had to adapt if she wanted to place his face exactly where she wanted it.

A shift to the left and some more downward pressure and her body was humming.

"Ummmm, sweet and indulgent, just like I remember." Ben spoke against her flushed pussy, adding a new layer to her pleasure. That vibration damn near sent her over the edge. The only thing pulling her back was the momentary thought of how he'd gotten better. She had no right to wonder, but she did all the same.

Her thoughts must have translated through her body language as Benton stopped feasting and met her eyes over the slight swell of her stomach.

"Where." He thrust his finger. "Did." He crooked his finger just right to stroke that secret spot inside her he'd only just discovered a few months before it all went sideways. "You. Go?" The stroking continued, but he dropped his mouth and took her swollen bud between his teeth, never breaking eye contact.

"Somewhere that I had no right to, and it doesn't matter." Her breathless answer caused his eyes to narrow. He released her clit and dragged his tongue from his finger right back to it, suckling and nibbling it until she crashed into ecstasy.

"Ah…ah…ahhhhhhhh." When she was skiing down the backside of her orgasmic slope, Ben climbed up her body and swiftly entered her then stilled with a groan of his own pleasure.

"We will talk about that later, for now, I'm going to fuck you so thoroughly, the couple in six-eighteen will need a shower and a smoke."

Ben pumped into her body with a vengeance. But it didn't seem to be enough for either of them. He reached down with first one arm, then the other and caught her knees to bring them to rest on his shoulders. Planting his elbows by her head, he continued his brutal pace.

It felt like he couldn't get deep enough. As if he were trying to fuse them together. Melt them down with friction then let them solidify as one.

For an eternity, she hovered on the razor's edge of soaring into the clouds in bliss. Each time her breathing would speed up and her body started to clench, Ben would hold himself still inside her and cluck his tongue. "Not yet, Cookie." Then he'd kiss her senseless.

"Oh." Shock flowed through her as Benton rolled while holding her in place so when he landed on his back, she was sitting straight up like a cowgirl. She untucked her knees from his shoulders to rest them at his side.

She quirked her eyebrow at the smug look and one-hundred-watt smile that graced his handsome face. Her answer was that seductive bite of his lip and his hands abandoning her body.

When he levered up and quickly tasted her nipple, she threw her head back and ground down on him. God, his body felt amazing and with the past melted away, it felt healing. His supple lips disappeared just as fast as they appeared and he was relaxed back on the pillow with his toned arms folded under his head.

"Giddyup." This playful Ben was new; maybe their time apart was good for him. As much as she hated to admit it, it was kind of good for her too.

Slapping his chest playfully, she left her hands there and started a slow roll of her hips. "Oh, is that how it's going to be?"

"Yeah, baby girl, that's how it's going to be." Ben gripped her hips—his fingers digging in rough enough to leave marks—and it amped her up. "I want you to make us both come so hard, our backs crack. Think you can handle it?"

He was dragging her back and forth on his cock, and it was stroking all her spots just right, so if she let him continue, it would be her coming with a crack and him left behind.

She dropped her body to his and spoke against his lips. "The real question is, can you handle it?" A quick kiss was all she had time for as she levered up and spun her body around while still impaled on his cock. It was his turn to make a bombing run.

"Fuck, baby girl, you are not fucking going there. Are you trying to kill me?" But the pleasure threading his voice and his hands returning to her hips told her he would die happy.

Using his muscular thighs for traction, she held tight and rode them both to ecstasy. When they were on the cusp of coming, Ben sat up, pressing his chest to her back and holding her down on his cock. A few grinds and they both shouted in pleasure before falling to their sides.

Spooning and still connected, Ben's full lips left barely-there kisses on her neck until he drifted off and slipped from her body.

He gripped her breast in a position they used to sleep in all the time. Right before sleep claimed him, he professed his love and tears sprang to her eyes.

Was there really a chance for them? After all the bullshit and the anger? After her deception with the rooms, *which he knows nothing about…yet?*

There was something she needed to do first. A piece of the past she needed to shed. With a little finesse, she was able to slip from the bed without waking Ben from his sex-induced stupor.

She snagged her purse and bag and locked herself in the bathroom. She adjusted the temp in the tub to perfection, but before getting in, she opened her purse. Her hand went straight to the compartment with the photo.

She unfolded it for the last time and took in Ben's chiseled features, softened in sleep. Treena draped across his broad chest with her fake tits pressed into his bicep. Her slutty smirk as she snapped the cancerous selfie.

It had worked. The cancer spread from her broken heart to her soul and crept outward, until it poisoned and strangled everything good they'd ever had.

As much as she still hated the image glaring back at her, it didn't hold the same power it once had. Not that cheating should ever be taken lightly, but there was a lot to be said about forgiveness. They were young. If they couldn't make mistakes then, when could they?

Forgiveness? Something she never thought she'd be able to extend to him without a confession.

Something she never dreamed she'd offer herself. It wasn't her fault he strayed, so forgiveness wasn't warranted there. However, her own actions that pushed him away and her reactions to suspicions did warrant it, and she accepted it.

It felt as if Ben had forgiven her too, so how could she not accept the same for herself. *Now if he can forgive me for the new mistakes I've made.*

Tracing the line of his jaw's likeness, she cried one last time before tearing the photo in half and half again and dropping it in the wastebasket.

Ray hugged her knees tight after she entered the cooling tub. She wasn't crying for either of their actions, but for the cost of it all. They'd lost almost an entire year and more.

For the first time since that Wednesday night last winter, she allowed her hand to drift along her stomach, back and forth below her navel. A cost she'd never dreamed she'd pay, a cost Ben didn't know *he'd* paid.

The memories were so vivid, she felt the cramps and saw the blood. The helplessness she'd felt then paralyzed her now. When the doctor told her their baby was gone, she'd rubbed her stomach like she could wish their child back into her uterus.

She'd lost their child, and she hadn't even gotten up the nerve up to tell him she was pregnant. Ray had only known of the baby for two months. By then, she was at the end of the first trimester and it had been time to tell him. To wait any longer, pain or not, would have been so wrong.

She had finally come to terms with them not being R & B but had accepted they could still be good parents as long as Treena wasn't a factor in their unconventional duel family plan.

She'd been denied the chance when she miscarried. When she was discharged to go home, she rubbed her belly one last time, swallowed her tears, and left.

The devastation of what had been lost pulled her into a depression that she thought she'd never claw her way out from. It wasn't until Ben called because their mutual friends had been worried about her. The concern in his voice was just too much. While he had a right to know, she simply couldn't share that agony with him.

Her pain had been so consuming, she didn't know how to dump that on him. She promised herself she'd tell him, but then one month turned to two. Spring turned to summer. Labor Day turned to Christmas.

When he suggested this excursion, she took that as a sign it was time, but then seeing him changed so much. How could she wipe that smile from his face, steal the joy he managed to find without her by digging up the past.

Now that they'd slept together, there was no way she could *not* tell him. He deserved to know. She turned it over in her mind until the water got cold, but the approach didn't come to her. For now, she'd accept all the things she could and figure out the best time to drop that news.

It needed to be soon because if her car was ready tomorrow, they'd resume their trip, and the last thing he needed was that kind of news on the way to meet someone who could change his life. So, it was either tonight, or wait until after, which Ben would see as a fresh betrayal of their new-found whatever this was.

As she toweled off, she started thinking of a way to get out of the room for the day. If they stayed, they would just end up making love again and that wouldn't do. They needed to get reacquainted with each other, and not just physically.

All problems couldn't be fixed with sex, no matter how awesome it was. Also, she needed an opportunity to talk with Ben. Let him know she had let the past go and to let him in on some of it.

She donned her most casual outfit and pulled her hair back in a ponytail. Skipping the makeup, she met her reflection. That simple act had been difficult for a time in her life.

Toward the last part of their relationship, and for months after, looking in the mirror caused her physical pain. The chunky soft person staring back at her never failed to bring her to tears. It had taken time and the loss of her child to be able to accept her body, flaws and all.

It wasn't her body that had caused Ben to stray. His choices were his choices, and while she may have contributed to them, people were ultimately responsible for their own behavior. When she finally accepted that truth, she began to change the way she viewed the past and the future.

Time to face that potential future now. Using her cell, she dialed the front desk and asked a few questions about the area. Same was as excited about her plans as she was.

With another pep talk to her reflection, she sighed and exited the bathroom, hoping for a nice day with Ben doing something she knew they'd both enjoy.

The sight that greeted her robbed her ability to think or speak. Ben was laid back with the sheet barely covering his mid-section. The rest of his tight, toned body was on display, and she devoured him with her eyes.

One arm was behind his head and the other hand rested on his abs, but it was heading south. It dipped below the sheet and stroked his cock. She tore her gaze from the hypnotic sight and visually tracked the length of his body. When it reached his face, he winked and bit his lip. The hand under the sheet paused it's slow up and down motion to raise the white linen in invitation.

Ben was already primed and ready to go again. As much as Ray wanted to say yes, toss her clothes and jump back into bed, she knew it wasn't what would serve them best in the long run.

Ray wasn't made of stone and couldn't resist plopping on the bed and leaning down to taste his lips. It wasn't the frenzied kisses they'd shared earlier; this was their hearts touching through their lips.

With regret, she broke the kiss and stared into his eyes for what felt like an eternity. Falling into his gaze had always caused a time lapse for her, one she thoroughly enjoyed.

"As *hard* as that offer is to resist, I was thinking a more, clothes-on activity."

Ben pulled her down on top of him and began peppering her with kisses. "Where's the fun in that?

Naked activities are so much more..." Ben nipped her breast through her shirt. "Rewarding."

Putting an end to this playfulness was almost impossible, but spending time with Ben...dressed, would be rewarding in a different way.

"I think spending the day just hanging out and getting to know each other again will be even more rewarding." She could tell she'd won the argument. Her victory was written in the chocolate depths she was in danger of sinking into.

Ben leaned up, gripped her neck, and kissed her once more. When his lips retreated and his hand slid forward to cradle her cheek, she knew if he asked her to spend the day in bed again, she'd cave. "I think that sounds heavenly. What did you have in mind?"

When he threw off the sheet and strode bare-assed and fully erect to his duffle, she damn near swallowed her tongue.

"Oh, um, I found the perfect thing. There's a hidden ghost town not that far from here, and Sam said he'd drop us off then pick us up when we are tired of hiking around, no problem. What do you think?" She didn't really need to ask; she knew she had him hooked at the mention of ghost town.

They shared a love of history in general, but especially from the mining era and stuff like that. "What do I think?" Ben came back to the bed and lifted her to her feet. "I think it's perfect, just like you. Why don't you order some sandwiches from the diner while I take a quick shower, and we can have a lunch pioneer style?"

"Sam is handling it. Go get clean and we'll get a move on. You're burning daylight." She playfully slapped his ass, as there was a knock on the door.

Ben hit the bathroom, and Ray opened the door. A beautiful native looking woman with a cart full of cleaning supplies and linens greeted her. "Hi, you must be Rayna. I'm Shelly, the one and only housekeeper extraordinaire here at Chance."

Shelly grabbed towels from her cart and went to go around Ray. "Oh, I'll take those. Thanks, Shelly, but this is all we need for now."

"Sure, do you want me to come back later?"

"Um, we don't really need anything but the towels. Thanks." Shelly just stood there. Either she took her job seriously or didn't really get subtle hints. "We are on our way out for the day, so…" Ray trailed off and tossed her head back toward the bathroom.

The housekeeper winked. "Not a problem, I'll come back later." With that, she turned her cart and headed back the way she came. They didn't really need her to come back later, but at least she was gone for now.

Something scratched at the back of her mind. She watched the housekeeper as she pushed her cart down the broken walkway and into what she could only assume was the storage room.

When she exited, she tossed her leg over the back of a bike with a man who was waiting and sped off.

Strange. If all the rooms are full, why not visit any of the other ones? They weren't on the end, so Ray had to assume they weren't her last scheduled room.

She shook off her questions and headed to the bathroom with the towels. She'd used the last one for her hair, so Ben would need them. Knocking felt a little distant considering he'd just been inside her, but barging in felt too familiar, assumptive. Her cheeks heated at the memory of him pumping into her body.

"Ben, I have towels for you."

"Come in, Cookie. I won't bite...unless you beg me to."

Rayna rolled her eyes as she opened the door. Ben stood in the middle of the floor, hands on his hips, and naked as the day he was born.

He really was an absolutely beautiful man. Entering the bathroom, she offered up the stack of towels. Ben stepped forward and closed the door with one hand, while he grabbed the towels with the other and placed them...somewhere.

All Ray could do was stare as if it had been a million years since she'd laid eyes on him. Ben used one finger to close her gaping jaw. "Damn, baby girl, if you keep that mouth open like that, I'll be obliged to fill it."

Ben feasted on her lips while his hand slipped into her pants. Her body was humming for his touch, and she almost went off when his finger grazed her clit. "One for the road, Ray? The ghost town will still be there."

How could she say no to him when he was making her body sing so loud, she couldn't hear herself think. "Okay, just a quickie, but..."

Ben didn't give her a chance to finish her sentence. The second *okay* left her mouth, he pulled her leggings down far enough to access her aching pussy and thrust into her, slamming them into the back of the door.

He was still wet from the shower, and it made for an odd sensation. Hot, wet skin in places and clothes blocking others while their bodies rocked violently together.

It took very little time and his name was echoing off the tile walls. Ben followed her into bliss with a raspy, "Rayna."

After a few moments of leaning against the door and panting, Ray kissed his shoulder and awkwardly shuffled over to the tissue to clean up. *Nothing worse than pulling up your pants with cum running down your leg to go for a hike.* The thought made her cheeks flush yet again.

Awkwardness overtook her. It wasn't what they'd done exactly, but maybe because she had truly let herself go and live in the moment. No thought of the future or consequences or pasts or being good enough, just his cock and her aching need.

That was new territory for her. Even earlier, she held a bit of control and coherent thought. Letting go was liberating and terrifying. Humor was how she dealt with discomfort. "Well, now that we've load-tested the door maybe I should bill Megan and Sam for the service." She quit the bathroom with a strained laugh and waited for Ben on the couch that wasn't really a couch.

CHAPTER 6

Ben could tell Ray was uncomfortable. He hated that he'd had a hand in that.

The sex had been mind-blowing; Ben was sure that wasn't it. He would've felt it had it been wrong. And what they'd just shared was anything but wrong. It was definitely something else. For a moment, he wondered if Bud had gotten a hold of her and said something. *No, surely she would've been pissed and led with that.* As much as he hated to be on the receiving end, Ray didn't pull punches as a rule. It was his own guilt in that area that was gnawing at his gut.

He tried to put himself in her shoes and wondered how he would react. After he reflected on that scenario, her thoughts were no clearer to him. He would see it completely different than he was sure she would. Ben would find it flattering if she went that extra mile to spend time with him. Thinking outside the box to gain a few extra hours together would mean she wanted him back enough to take a risk.

Of course, the Ray he knew wouldn't think that way. She'd probably feel betrayed...again. Even though he hadn't slept with Treena, he had betrayed her.

Ben missed all the signs their relationship was in trouble, that *Ray* was in trouble. He was so wrapped up in going pro that when she started down the path of thinking she was fat and crash dieting and trying diet pill after diet pill, he'd missed the dangers. He loved her curves, but he'd also loved when she started losing some. Ben just loved her, no matter what, but he'd failed her.

Of all the ways he'd botched things, the fact he'd let Treena so deep in her head was one he regretted just a bit more. Once that she-devil found footing with demeaning Ray about her weight, she was able to convince her they'd slept together somehow.

Even though Ben had forgiven Rayna and let that shit go, he still didn't know how Treena had managed to convince Ray so thoroughly of his supposed unfaithfulness.

Just another thing I blame myself for.
No more.

That was the vow he made to himself. No more hurt, no more bullshit, no more Treenas. Ray would never feel that way about herself again. He'd spend every day for the rest of his life convincing her of how amazing, beautiful, and worthy she was.

Even if they didn't get a second chance at the life they'd planned so long ago, Ben would not have her doubting herself like she had.

Ray deserved to be loved, especially by herself, and Ben would do what he could to ensure that.

However, he damn near choked on the thought of her being with another man. Having his children, smiling at him over morning coffee, sucking his cock the way she used to Ben's.

"Fuck." Ben scrubbed his hands down his face and shoved those thoughts from his head. Yes, he wanted her to be happy above all else, but he wanted her happy with him.

God knows, she's the only person I'll ever be happy with. Only her. Now, I need to make that happen. While she loved his body, she loved his mind and sense of humor more. What better place to showcase those things than hiking through a ghost town. He quickly pulled up a few facts about where they were headed and nodded to his reflection.

Operation Win Back Rayna was a go.

He covertly snagged a few things from his duffle.

They were headed for the diner when Megan and Sam exited the office with two big backpacks. Sam raised 'em high. "Got the grub. Y'all ready for a ghost town adventure?"

Megan patted Sam's arm as they approached, causing him to lower them. "I hope you don't mind, but we thought we'd join you. Of course, we won't be anywhere near where you decide to explore, but Sam and I have a soft spot for a few places out there, and I thought we'd have a picnic of our own."

The four of them headed to Sam's vehicle and started loading up the food. "Really, you won't see us. I promise," Megan all but whispered to Ben as they made their way to the passenger's side. "Just a hint, take her to the second building along the trail. It has just enough of a roof to offer a little protection, but an adequate amount of sunlight gets through. It's fairly clean and safe. People go there a lot and leave things for the next visitors."

Ben thanked Megan for her tip and opened the door for her.

The drive was interesting. Megan basically knew the history backward and forward, and Sam told tales of exploring the mines, caves, and old buildings in the area.

Ben kept his attention on Ray, no matter what the conversation. She was absolutely stunning with her light hair in a ponytail, no makeup, and practical clothes.

When she pulled her lip balm from her pocket and circled her mouth twice with it, his cock sprang to life. How could they not be meant for each other when the mere act of protecting her lips was seductive to him.

He failed to notice the car had stopped. "Everything else is on foot unless you've got a horse or ATV I don't know about." Sam's deep voice pulled him from his dirty thoughts.

They exited the vehicle and started putting on packs. "One is lunch. The other has some basics in it including GPS, SAT phone, flares, rope, and carabineers, stuff like that in case of an emergency. You can never be too careful. I'm putting the spare keys on the tire in case you get back before us, you can stay warm while you wait. Meet back by seven?"

"Sounds good. Thanks for this, guys. I really needed to get out of that room." Ray's words pierced his heart. Was he the reason she needed out so desperately? He sure as hell hoped not.

Shouldering the lunch since it was heavier, he helped Ray put the emergency gear on her back.

The conversation was light as they made their way past a building that had interesting machinery in it but was impassable. One step inside and it seemed likely to collapse. They took guesses on what the machine once was. With it partially obstructed by the fallen roof, neither really had a clue but they enjoyed guessing all the same.

Ben took a chance and seized her hand in his, interlacing their fingers as the trail evened out. "This is nice."

"Yeah," Ray agreed. "I have to admit, I've missed you like a part of my own body these last months."

The impromptu confession caught them both off guard. It was obvious Ray never meant to say it, at least not to him, and Ben was practically vibrating with excitement. Her words settled deep in his soul.

"I've missed you too, Cookie. And spending this time with you has been damn near indescribable, but I say we enjoy the day with no pressure. Just R & B hanging out and getting reacquainted with no expectations. And when we get back to the room tonight, we can see where it leads."

Oh, Ben had expectations, big ones, long-term ones, but he wasn't about to drop that on her right now. He wanted her to focus on the moment, not worry about expectations and thinking three steps ahead.

Ray didn't do well under that kind of pressure. If she thought his behavior was a ploy to pass the time between her thighs or to seek absolution, then all would be lost. She valued authenticity, and he was going to give it to her and let her come to her own conclusions about how great R & B 2.0 could be. As long as the past was left there and the future stretched out in front of them, he believed they could make a go of it.

With any luck, when he introduced her to his potential client as his fiancée, and when they visited her family, no lies would be told nor stand between them. They would be an actual couple. *Fingers crossed.*

Ben didn't give a shit about whether she believed him about Treena or not, he'd made his peace with their past. Although, he did think she needed to believe him for her own peace of mind.

The problem was, how could he approach that in a way she didn't feel like he was just trying to clear his own name?

They hiked silently, hand in hand, for a good twenty minutes. Passing collapsed cave entrances and dilapidated shafts.

It was companionable and gave him plenty of time to ponder a few things. Even when they stopped to take a few selfies with breathtaking backgrounds, her hand ended up firmly back in his and they enjoyed each other's company.

Ben could see the second structure up ahead and Megan was right, it was in pretty good condition. From the sight of the first one and the photos he glanced at in the bathroom earlier, the second building was definitely the best this mountain had to offer.

"Oh, look." Ray removed her hand to point and clap. "That looks like a great place to eat, and I'm starving."

The mere mention of food had his cock hardening in his pants. The last time they'd eaten, they ended up naked.

Ben didn't want to steal her thunder at discovering a place for their picnic, so he kept his mouth closed about Megan's recommendation and eyed her ass as she jogged ahead.

Ray entered without hesitation before he got there. "Oh, my gosh, Ben. There are candles with lighters, and chairs, and oh, a book of poetry. It's like a little lunch spot just for us."

When he entered, she already had the candle lit atop of the industrial spool set up as a makeshift table. Two aluminum chairs were on either side, and sure enough, a well-worn book sat there as well.

They both let their backpacks down and began rummaging through them. As Ben started removing food and placing it on the table, Ray pulled out the fuzziest looking blanket he'd even seen from her pack. "Oh, but look, do you mind eating on the floor? It would seem a shame to let this go to waste."

"That's a perfect idea." After setting the food out on the spool, Ben uncorked the wine and poured two glasses. He offered Ray one after she'd carefully spread the blanket.

"To first loves." Ray tapped her plastic glass against his and held up the book. Her indication was obviously their shared love of poetry, but Ben wasn't buying that as her only meaning.

"And second chances," he added. It felt like a moment out of a Hallmark Christmas movie.

Her nose was pinked from the cold, and had a little bite to it, but they weren't completely frozen. *Thank god for the mild Nevada winters.* But other than the lack of snow, it was right off the small screen.

Their tasty lunch was all gone and they were nearing the bottom of the bottle when Ben got an idea. A way to get to know each other…again, but without the pressure, or time that process usually involved.

"Ray, remember how we used to play twenty questions with all our friends to figure out what they did over the summer?"

Her laugh echoed oddly off the not so solid walls, and Ben couldn't help but smile. "Oh, my God, yes, used to do it every year since…forever. It was the only time I complained that we went to Florida every summer." Ray finished her glass and offered up the rest of the wine between the two. "You want to play again, for old time's sake?"

Ben leaned in and dropped a quick kiss on her nose. "Not exactly for old time's sake, but to see what we've been up to this *summer*, so to speak. I want to know what you've been doing, learn how you've changed. If nothing else, we're friends and I want to know my friend. As much as I miss all the benefits of being R & B." His gaze raked her body, leaving no doubt to what benefits he spoke of. "I miss my best friend like crazy. You've been a part of my life since middle school. I miss that, don't you?"

Ray set her glass aside, cupped his cheeks, and Ben burrowed into her, allowing his eyes to drift closed as he savored her touch. "You have no idea." He opened them as her lips descended to his in a closed-mouth, but very emotional kiss.

When she drew back, Ben saw warring emotions and pain in her tear-glossed olive eyes. "But you don't need to ask. I have things I am ready to share with you, even if you don't like them."

That sounded both ominous and promising. "I have things to tell you, too."

"First" —she leaned over and snagged the poetry book— "read something for me, please? You know I love the sound of your voice, and I kinda need some flowery words right now."

Her gaze dropped to her lap as he took the book from her hand. She spoke softly and to herself, but Ben heard. "I miss your poetry, so raw and edgy. I'd take a Benton Davis over a Lord Byron or Dickinson any day."

Ben blushed. Even with his dark skin, he felt positive she could see the flame of his cheeks. Ray and his mother were the only two people alive who knew he wrote poetry. It was not a part of him he embraced, except for them.

He thumbed through the book and stopped on a page about midway. He lifted the book slightly in her direction. "Well, Cookie, you get what you get…then it's share time."

Ben cleared his throat and began.

"grays turn black with the march of time
    contrast the past and it's too late
the haunts and ghosts fly swiftly onward
    blackening their wake and tempting fate

seeds of discord grow so fast
    blocking out a crystal view
thickened trunks and roots sunk deep

VERLENE LANDON

is what is seen really true

it's in the gray that we ponder
    looking closer for what is real
black is black and that is that
    but 'tis not in black we truly feel

black is nothing and nothing in black
    even pain and a heart torn wide
are but genuine in the gray
    but in the black the truth does hide

thoughts appear so stark and true
    cloaked in the black of the past
real truth clings to the bits of gray
    if we can manage to hold fast"

Ben closed the book and looked into Ray's transparent face. She was stunned; that was clear, but was she moved by the words or—

"That was so not in that book. I recognize a Benton James Davis original when I hear one. Did you just make that up?"

The look of amazement on her face had the lie poised on his tongue. He wanted her to always be wowed by him but lying was not the way to go. Not when he still had one to confess.

"No. I wrote that shortly after we broke up. I recited it to myself more often than I care to admit. It was my way of clinging to the reality we lived instead of looking back with such black and white views that the untrue might seem real and reality seem like a lie. I wanted to remember everything accurately, even the pain." Ben left it at that.

There was so much more to say, but he could tell she got it. There was no need to reiterate what he was thinking when he wrote it or what it meant and still means to their situation; she just got it, got *him*.

That made his heart soar. He wasn't a great poet or even a good one, but his lines were simple and from the heart. Even if a middle schooler with mediocre rhyming skills could match the majority of what he wrote, the fact that he wrote them at all meant a lot to him.

Ben reached into his pocket and pulled a worn piece of paper from it and extended it to her. She took the square of paper with trembling fingers and gingerly unfolded it. He watched her eyes. Ben knew what her eyes were seeing. Faded ink of the words he'd just recited. A last-minute grab from his duffle.

When he shoved it into his pocket on the way out of the room, he couldn't imagine how he could show it to her, even though he was desperate to. But the old book of poetry and her request provided a perfect opportunity. *It was kismet.*

The look on Ray's barely freckled face spoke to how much his words touched her, too. He couldn't hold back any longer. After tossing the book aside, he knelt in front of her.

Wrapping her hair in his hand, Ben maneuvered her mouth to the precise angle he wanted before he attacked her lips. Something about their raw vulnerability in that moment forced him to dominate and own her kiss.

Swallowing her moans was ecstasy; they tasted of reconciliation and salvation. This wasn't something they'd explored prior, domination, but they damn sure would going forward.

Ben ended the kiss and felt empty, so he dove back in for another sample of her. This time, when he pulled back, they were both panting, her eyes glazed over in bliss.

He took a mental snapshot before he encircled her in his arms, and he noted a change in her almost immediately. A tension tightened her body, and he practically felt an emotional distancing.

That will not do.

CHAPTER 7

Rayna was adrift on a turbulent sea. She wanted to cling to the only stable thing within sight on the emotional swells and tidal waves.

Ben.

She felt herself being pulled under but there was a certain amount of peace to it. She wanted to drown in all of this, in *him*. Everything about Ben pulled at her. From his silky voice speaking heartfelt words, to the sincerity swirling in his whiskey brown eyes.

Time slowed as they just stared at each other. Their breathing had already returned to normal, and neither made a move to repeat the kiss. Instead, her fingers ghosted over every angle of his face. When his eyes slipped closed, she caressed his lids too, and his face took on a look of contentment.

Her thumbs traced his brows then she walked her fingertips down his jawline. Her explorations stilled, and she held his cheeks.

"Ben. I don't even know where to start. I found it impossible to let us go. Even if that meant holding on to pain and anger because it was something I could cling to that was from us."

The words paused, and she resumed her tactile reading of his features. This time, she enjoyed feeling the silk of his full lips and the angle of his nose, lingering again to cup his cheeks.

"It took me letting go of you but holding the pain to survive. And I was doing fine until you called. I thought I could do this with you and not get attached, but the minute you sat in the passenger's seat and changed my music to eighties pop, I knew I'd never be happy again without you."

"Ray—"

"Please, Ben, just let me at least get a small confession out of the way before I chicken out for good."

Ben nodded his acquiescence. She could see the tornado building in his gaze—good and bad swirling together, looking to touch down—but he quelled the storm because she'd asked it. That spoke volumes.

"Once we'd been on the road together, talking and joking…anyway, I'm sorry, but when we got to the motel, I tried to get Sam and Megan to help trick you into staying in the same room with me. Turns out there weren't other rooms, but now I'm not so sure they didn't take my idea and run—"

Her words ended when his lips crashed into hers. Ben practically ate the remaining syllables. When he pulled back, he had that million-watt smile turned up high, and it shifted to a wolfish grin. "Don't you dare apologize. I am beyond flattered that you'd go through that much trouble just to spend time with me."

He bent to her ear and took the lobe into his mouth, pulling a groan of pleasure from her. He released it and spoke with that smoky nightclub voice. "I have a confession of my own. We could be on our way right now, but I told Bud we'd deal with the car later so I could have a few more precious, if stolen, hours with you."

They both stilled at his words. All the oxygen felt as if it had been sucked from the cabin they occupied. "When did he call?" she asked in a shaky voice. The answer to that question would determine how flattered she was. Did he decide he enjoyed her company and want to spend time with her before they did the horizontal tango or after because he wanted more sex?

Rayna knew she was wrong reducing it to that, but a slight insecurity still lingered. Even though she fought it, it was something that wouldn't go away overnight. Her head said let it go, but her heart still held the echo of past pain.

"This morning before you came back with breakfast. But if I'm being honest, I would've done the same thing if he'd called five minutes after we checked in or five minutes ago."

Ben withdrew just enough for their eyes to clash. "I love you, Ray. I never stopped loving you, and this breakdown was the best thing to happen to us in a long time. It's like even fate knew we needed a smack in the back of the head."

A playful smack in the back of the head is exactly what she gave him. "Oh my God, you're such a jerk." Rayna didn't mean it one bit, but she'd always enjoyed these moments before. They'd laugh, wrestle, and play fight. It was flashes of time like that she remembered as having made their relationship fun.

All the pressure of finals, games, just being a couple who looked the way they looked all melted away in the moments like that. She was lightly smacking his chest when he caught her hands and held them to his pecs. Pecs she couldn't help but gently squeeze. Ben reacted immediately; his eyes became hooded, and she could practically track the passion as it coursed through his body.

"Um, Cookie, don't start anything out here you're not willing to finish out here." His meaning was clear. He was getting to the point he would risk Sam and Megan catching them in the act if she were game.

Another new and exciting side to Ben.

"Besides, I'm not the one who tried to trap a poor innocent man in a room for her own sexual gratification." The mirth glimmered in his eyes, and his laugh boomed in the atmosphere.

"Yeah, you couldn't even pull that one with a straight face." For a wisp of time, they shared the humor in the situation.

Both wanted reconciliation, but neither were sure if the other did, so each resorted to some not-so-aboveboard ways to do it.

Ray was still laughing when Ben took on a more serious mien. Her heart thudded wildly before ceasing in her chest. Was he about to bring up *the* subject? Having accepted and moved on was one thing, talking about it was quite another. If that topic came up out here, so would the other. She really wanted to wait until they were back at Chance where she could break down to talk about.

"Ben—"

With a gentle finger, he shushed her. "Ray, nothing you have to say can change what *I* want to say, so save it for after, please?"

She didn't exactly agree, but she was too emotionally frozen in place to argue.

"It's obvious we belong together. So what do you say, we get the car from Bud and drive into Vegas. We could be married before the lunch buffet opens tomorrow?"

Oh, my God, oh, my God, oh, my God.

Her mind was reeling. It was the most beautiful proposal, but how could she…

"Ben, you should hold that proposal for after we get back to the room. We need to…I…there are things you should know before you make a decision like that."

Ben's face darkened with what she thought was anger, but his words told her otherwise.

"Ray. Is it still the same wedge as before? I thought, well, never mind what I thought, but that is the past and I'll—"

Holding his face with both hands, she watched the pain swell in his eyes. "Ben, no. It's not that. It's…something I need to tell you. Something you deserve to know, but...it's something I don't want to get into out here. I promise as soon as we get back to the room, we'll discuss everything."

She tasted their tears when she pressed her lips to his. "And if you don't want to recant your proposal and go screaming back home, I'd be happy to discuss it with you then."

Ben kissed her soundly and pulled her to her feet. He started packing up their stuff and encouraging her to do the same. "Well, then. Let's get a move on because I want a yes before the night is over, and if that can only happen back at the motel, well, I'll carry you back down the trail on my damn back if I have to."

His words were light, and his face sparked with love, but there was a shadow lurking in him that wasn't there before. One that spoke of so many dark emotions, she wasn't sure which would rear its head.

Only one way to find out—tell him the truth and let the chips fall where they may.

She wished like hell she could put him out of his misery, but she couldn't, not here. As lovely as this day had been, this was not a place she could get into the most painful time of her life.

As they made their way down the trail, she mourned the loss of the old Ben and the new one. Ray knew as soon as she shared the miscarriage with him, he would cease to just be Ben and become a man who'd lost a child. If she could spare him that pain, she would. But if they were to have any chance, everything had to come out.

Even the shit with Treena.

She didn't need him to say it anymore, that was true, but they both needed to accept the whole situation and all the fallout that resulted from it.

Megan and Sam were waiting for them when they arrived at the vehicle. *How had they passed the cabin without being seen?*

The gleam in Megan's eye told Ray they *had* at least seen *them*, but they'd obviously passed before the mood shifted.

The other woman was practically jumping up and down. Ray didn't know how to tell her without bringing the entire mood down. Luckily, Ben came to her rescue. He always did.

After he took both backpacks and deposited them in the back, he draped his arm around her shoulder and addressed the other couple.

"I can tell by the look on your face you overheard my proposal. We are saving the yes and the celebration for back at the hotel. After all, it is what brought us back together, right? So, we promise to come back after Elvis hitches us in Vegas." Ben added just enough humor to really sell it.

He kissed her temple. If Megan and Sam thought there was any trouble in paradise, their faces didn't show it. They were both beaming with excitement. Ben was always a smooth-talker. Ray thought he missed his calling as a lawyer.

"Not to get technical, but it was a broken drive shaft tha—"

Megan interrupted by pulling Rayna into a hug. "A broken drive shaft that brought you to my hotel, so…"

The redhead released her and grabbed Ben in a quick hug before returning to Sam's side where she seemed so content to be.

"Congratulations, you two. And, on your way back, your stay is on us. We'll even make sure *your* room is available."

Ray was starting to get a little uncomfortable with the whole situation. Especially since she'd convinced herself Ben would have second thoughts after.

Opening the door, Ben ushered her into the backseat with a quick word of thanks to Sam, then entered the other side. The windows were cracked, and Ray eavesdropped on the other couple's conversation, letting their happiness wash over her. She was hoping it was contagious.

This was the day she'd dreamed about since they broken up. A perfect reconciliation, but with the secret looming over her head she couldn't find it in her bruised heart to be happy and expect the best.

"I told you the hotel is magical." Megan's tinkling voice broke through her thoughts.

"Magic had nothing to do with it, babe. That was all them…with a little push from us."

I knew it. Sam lied about the rooms.

Her hand flew to her mouth to stifle the giggle that was bubbling up inside her.

Fate was all she could think of.

Fate in the form of a broken drive shaft that caused Bud to bring them to Chance Inn on 2nd—their second chance—and to a couple of hotel owners who seemed to be so deep in love they wanted the world to feel the same. To the point they would lie to help strangers.

A honeymoon suite from the seventies that brought them together physically and somehow gave Ray the means to let go of the one thing holding her back.

A ghost town cabin that just happened to have a poetry book, affording Ben the catalyst he needed to share his deepest feelings.

If Ray believed in magic, she would've had to agree with Megan.

Ben leaned across the backseat and kissed her sweetly while lacing their fingers together.

"Stop fretting so much, Cookie. I'm not worried about what you need to tell me. I love you, and nothing you can say will make me take back a single syllable I spoke today."

Her free hand immediately went to his handsome face. Something about touching him as much as she could always grounded her and made the mountains into molehills.

"I didn't say it before, because I was scared and thought it'd make the heartbreak more real if you decided to bolt, but you deserve the words. I, Rayna Beth Wilson, love you, Benton James Davis with my whole heart and always have. No matter where we go from here, where our paths may lead, together or apart, that will never change."

His smile was so blinding, if she hadn't already been in love with him, that smile alone would've stolen her heart.

*T*hank *fucking Christ. She said it. She actually said the words.* No vague whispered confession or simple I love you—Ray went above and beyond to let him know how much she cared, and his heart soared.

There wasn't a damn thing she could confess that would make him change his mind. They'd already lost enough time together as far as he was concerned, too damn much.

However, whatever it was weighed very heavy on Rayna and that wouldn't do. She'd been through enough bullshit, and he didn't want her to suffer so much as a hangnail or minor disappointment moving forward.

The whole trip back to the hotel, Ben racked his brain for answers and none came. What could be so bad it could hold her hostage like it was? How long has she lived with whatever it is?

Ben could only hope and pray it wasn't too long. He had to admit, it was amazing to hear her dismiss the infidelity thing after all the heartache and bullshit surrounding it with her needing that closure. A closure he'd been unable to give her in the form of a confession.

This, whatever this was, was different. He didn't know how or what, but he had to shoulder that pain for her. No matter what the secret, Ben would accept it, and they'd move on…together.

When they arrived at the hotel, Sam waved them off when they tried to help unload. "We got this. You two go celebrate. Oh, by the way, Bud called earlier. We told him to bring the car by in the morning. Hope that's okay, but we were headed out for the hike, and well, it kind of slipped my mind. If that's an issue for you, I can have him bring it tonight?"

They were already a few steps away by the time Sam finished. Ray untangled her hand and returned to the couple by the car. A small twinge of jealousy crept into his chest when Ray stood on her tiptoes and gave the big guy a peck on the cheek. "Slipped your mind, my ass." She dropped to the balls of her feet. "Thank you. Both of you."

She returned to Ben's side and grabbed his hand. Bringing it to her mouth, she just let it linger in front of her face as her gaze seemed to devour him. They continued on to their room.

"Do you mind if we shower first?"

Ben spun her around, and his answer came swiftly. "Yes, Cookie, I do mind. The longer you stall, the longer I have to wait for an answer from those enticing lips and the longer it will be before I can sink into your banging body."

It must really seem bad to her if the fear in her frightened stare is any indication. "Rayna, I love you. Let me share whatever it is with you. Let me carry your burdens."

She turned away from him but he could tell she was wringing her hands. "Remember you said that." Her words were mumbled, but he managed to make them out.

Ben heard her deep intake of breath and watched her shoulders slump even farther down before she turned back to him. Tears were running down her cheeks, and in that moment, he felt impotent. Powerless to take her pain and kiss away whatever was causing her tears.

"After we broke up, I sunk into a really bad place. A place I never want to visit again, but then a tiny ray of light entered my life. I was so happy, but before I could figure out how to reach out to you or deal with my own broken heart over, well, you know. I lost her. I lost our baby."

Her words hadn't really sunk in yet. All he knew were her tears had turned to a full-on bawl. She turned from him again, hugging her middle so tightly, he feared she'd pass out.

Did she say...

"It was my fault. I cried all day, every day. Then I would stare at that vile picture of you and Treena until my tears dried and I passed out from exhaustion."

"We...we made a baby?"

Ray spun around with anger glowing in her teary gaze, anger at herself.

"Yes, we did, but I was too childish to let all that go, and I lost her before I could even tell you. She was the size of a plum. I had her heartbeat committed to memory and I always will, but it's my fault you are not holding your daughter right now. ME! I—"

Ben couldn't take another minute of it. He scooped her up into his arms and dropped them onto the loveseat. He just held her while letting his own tears fall into her hair.

"I'm so sorry, Ben. So, so, sorry."

"Shush now, Ray. You have nothing to be sorry for. You dealt with that all by yourself and were still able to agree to do this trip, and you made love to me…I…You have nothing to apologize for, I should be the one begging for your forgiveness for not being there like I should've been."

Repeatedly kissing her head and shushing her didn't really help, but for some reason, it comforted him. He'd had a daughter, one he'd never get the pleasure of knowing, but one he got to mourn with her other parent. Something denied the woman he loved.

"Ray. I wish like hell that I had the perfect words, but I don't. I do know it's not your fault. I don't blame you, but I get why everything was amplified now. The…"

Words failed him so he just sat silent until her tears stopped. Something she said was nagging away at him, but how to bring it up was the question.

"So, I'm still a go for Elvis, after family and client, and then back here to this luxurious honeymoon suite. How about you?" Ray raised her head for the first time since her confession. Her eyes were red and swollen but most of the shadows lurking there were gone.

Even her shoulders seemed more erect with the weight gone. Ben had a good feeling about the future.

They both appeared to want the same thing, just neither was ready to put their selves out there after all that pain.

"Yeah." Ray swiped her eyes and then wound her arms around his neck. "If you still want to after everything, then yeah, let's do it. You know my dad will be thrilled. He loves you."

"And my mom, well, she'll still be my mom, but don't let that stop you." The laugh they shared at that was lighter than any they'd recently enjoyed.

"She's not that bad, Ben, at least not as bad as you like to think." They shared a claiming kiss.

Even though their mood had shifted slightly, the pain was still there. A pain that would always be there, but Ben tried to cling to the better feelings instead. But he had to address something. "I hate to ruin this moment, but can I ask what you meant by vile picture of that witch and me?" It was burning in his gut, flames licking at his heart. He had to know, even if it popped their little bubble.

The way Ray looked at him was confused, questioning. With a sad smile, she lifted herself off his lap and went to the bathroom. A string of curses followed a few seconds later.

"It was here, Ben, but now it's gone." She came out of the bathroom in a panic; she sounded almost grief stricken. "Shelly. She must've come back and emptied the trash. We have to go talk to her."

"Calm down. Just tell me, babe." He stood and rubbed her arms.

"It doesn't matter, Ben. Really, it—"

He pulled her into his chest. "It does matter, sweetheart. It mattered so much to you that you blamed yourself for losing our child. That means it matters."

"It was…it was a pic of you and Treena in bed. She sent it to me after we'd broken up as some sort of sick parting gift. She said it was of the first time y'all were together to remind me what a shallow person you were, and I was better off without you." Her tears returned with a vengeance, but Ben was pissed.

Ben put her at arm's length when her tears slowed. He needed her to see his face, the truth he hoped he could convey.

"I don't know what photoshop magic she did, but I never took a picture with her, in bed or otherwise."

"Ben—"

He turned and grabbed his cell phone. "Don't Ben me, I need you to know that isn't true. I don't need you to have that in the back of your mind. I damn sure don't want you thinking it was real."

Ben scrolled through his phone. Nothing. "Do you still have that bitch's number?"

Ray nodded. "I deleted her from my contacts, but I still have an old text."

"Babe, so much makes sense now. How could you believe me if you had what seemed like proof? I'm sorry I didn't protect you from her, but that ends now."

His finger shook and his anger boiled as he entered the numbers from Ray's screen into his phone. It was a test he never thought he'd have to face.

"You good with what I might need to say to get her to tell the truth?"

Ray nodded again but worried her lip. Ben knew this would be hard on her, but it would be even harder if she always believed what she saw with her own eyes. Forgiveness only goes so far.

He hit speaker mode, and they waited to hear the voice they both hated.

"Hello."

"Treena? Hey, it's Ben."

"Ben." She practically purred. "How come it took you so long to finally call me? What's it been now, a year? How have you been? Good, I hope? You know I never stopped thinking about you."

The words that were about to come out of his mouth lodged in his throat, choking him. "I never stopped thinking about you either, Treena."

She was practically giddy at his words. He held Ray's gaze the whole time and tried to apologize with his eyes.

"Oh, really? What is it you think about when I'm in that handsome head of yours?"

Here goes nothing. "I think about how we never got the chance to hook-up. I often wonder what it would've been like."

Ray made a gagging motion that almost caused him to laugh out loud.

"Well, you know what they say, it's never too late. I fantasized about what it would be like almost every day. Why don't—"

A roar of anger cut off the voice on the phone. "You fucking cunt. You orchestrated the whole thing. Where did you get the picture, huh?" Ray was seething.

"Ah, so this little phone call was a setup, huh? I had higher hopes for you, Ben. Oh—" Ray snatched the phone from his hand, ended the call, and kissed him senseless.

"Ray, you know you'll never know now."

"I know everything I need to know. I know I love you and you love me. I know you never slept with her. I know you wrote a poem to get through the darkness and that you lied about the car for a few more hours with me. I know that we are going to Vegas to get hitched by

Elvis. I know all I need to know. Now, make love to me like it's the first time."

Ben swiftly undressed them both and carried her to the bed, coming down on top of her. "The first time was awkward and not my best performance, let's go with another time if we're to recreate one."

Sliding down her body was a different experience now that he knew his child once resided there. He took his time suckling her breasts and kissing his way down the plane of her stomach. His hand lingered, noting, even if he couldn't see it, there was something missing now.

The words, *Not for long,* skated through his mind. Although they hadn't discussed a new life plan, they both previously wanted children. He wanted a child now more than anything, and he hoped Ray was on board.

"Um." He kissed the inside of one thigh, then the next. "I have a craving for cookies." He pierced her with his tongue and savored the flavor that was uniquely her. Her moans encouraged his path. Tonguing her cunt and clit, he couldn't wait for her to come down his throat.

Thrusting a finger into her caused her back to arch off the bed. "Oh, God, Ben." She gripped his head so tightly, he thought she might crush it. Another finger added and a well-placed bite and she was soaring with the angels. Before she had a chance to start her descent,

Ben crawled up her body and thrust into her waiting heat, prolonging the pleasure train she was riding.

He couldn't resist pounding into her like he was trying to drive her through the bed to the floor. When she clamped down on his cock, he realized she was in the throes of another orgasm. They'd never experienced that before, and her grasping body ripped his from him.

When the last of his orgasm receded, he spoke. "What do you think about making a baby, Cookie? If we just did, would you be okay with that?"

He rolled to the side but stayed firmly rooted inside her.

"Yeah, I'd be okay with that. It would be tough financially right now, but I think we can pull it off if we worked hard."

Ben dropped a kiss on her forehead and pulled her closer and began to pierce her with his cock in a slow build of passion. "I think so too, Cookie. Let's try again. You know what they say, practice makes perfect."

EPILOGUE

Rayna was putting on her earrings when Ben hugged her from behind. "I love it when you wear your hair up." He peppered kisses along the column of her neck. "You know how it turns me on." He growled and his kisses became bites.

The way he was still attracted to her after all they'd been through never ceased to amaze her. It was all she'd hoped for them and more. Turning in his arms ripped a groan from his throat as her hip brushed his hardened dick. Stretching up, she kissed his full lips and pulled back just enough to give him a wicked smile. But Ben liked to turn the tables. When his white teeth bit into his dark lower lip, it was her who groaned.

Ray rubbed his cock through his tux pants. Relishing the feel of it in against her palm. The fabric adding to the layers of tactile sensations for both of them.

"You know what that lip biting does to me. Why must you tease me so when I'm already dressed, and we have—" She looked at the bracelet on her wrist like a watch. The voice of her mother-in-law telling them Sam and Megan were here, told her what her bracelet could not. "To leave now or we'll be late."

It wouldn't do for Benton to miss his first client—the one who caused that fateful road trip—receiving the Offensive Player of the Year award. But that wasn't why she was practically giddy. Today was their two-year wedding anniversary.

Last year they spent their anniversary with a road trip back to the Chance Inn and went hiking and exploring with Sam and Megan in the same area they did when they got back together. Ben read a new original poem to her and everything. It was absolutely perfect.

This year, they were road tripping with their now best friends to Tombstone, Arizona instead. Same plan, just a different location. It was going to be an annual thing until they were too old to travel.

As much as she wanted him to bend her over the footboard of their bed and fuck her senseless, she abandoned that idea to be practical, *gulp*, responsible.

Those were words she used a lot over the last few years.

Ben's job afforded them a few luxuries they never expected after his professional career path was blocked. Like a house big enough for Benton's mother to live with them after a fire took everything from her. She and Ray were growing closer and more accepting of each other.

Ray got her dream job as a kindergarten teacher and Benton had signed all the clients he could manage. They had sensible cars that wouldn't leave them stranded on a lonely Nevada highway. They were brutally honest with their feelings so no big misunderstandings based on silence and retreat would plague them. No secrets.

Well, except one. Ray turned the hand on his cock toward her semi-flat belly hidden behind her sleek black dress. Her body hadn't started changing yet, not so anyone would notice, but she did.

Emotion caught in her throat and attempted to choke her. *These are changes I've been through before.* Thinking of the baby she lost still ripped her heart apart. But she was determined not to let that shadow this pregnancy.

She looked into chocolate eyes that changed her life and knew she wouldn't be alone no matter what the future held.

With a sigh of regret, she lifted both hands to Ben's neck and brought their lips together in a quick kiss. She planned to tell him tonight once they got to the hotel in Tombstone. Megan was super excited for them to see her hotel find. Supposedly the hotel was built like an old west town. Ray couldn't wait.

With a sigh of regret, she prepared to end their playtime. "It's time to go. Save that for later." Ray's hand dragged down his hard body to caress his cock once more before she turned for the door.

Downstairs, Megan and Sam waited with Ben's mother. They turned in unison as they descended the stairs. "So, let's get this show on the road, I'm anxious to get to Tombstone." Ben turned and waggled his eyebrows at Ray causing her to giggle. One hand flew to her mouth and the other gently caressed her belly. Ray greeted their guests and then dropped a kiss on his mother's cheek. All eyes were wide and on her except Ben's.

Uncomfortable with that much attention, she practically shouted, "What?"

Ben turned to see what everyone else was staring at. Ray lowered her own gaze to see what captured the room so thoroughly. *My hand? Why...*

She dropped the hand cradling her stomach protectively as soon as she realized her mistake. When she looked up, her eyes clashed with Ben's unreadable ones. Diverting her attention momentarily to the other faces, she knew the gig was up. Megan was practically vibrating and crying. The only person still slightly puzzled was Ben.

"Fuck it. I wanted this to wait until Tombstone, but since everyone here seems to be a freaking detective..." Ray stepped into Ben's personal space and looked up into his confused face. "What do you say we get to the awards ceremony, get on the road, and celebrate our last anniversary as two...Daddy?"

The confusion didn't seem to lessen, and Ben just stared into her eyes looking for answers. Ben's mom smacked him in the back of the head to snap him out of it. "Oh, for Christ's sake, I'm going to be a grandmother, son. Now step aside so I can give my daughter a hug."

Ben's mother didn't get the chance, he swept her up into his arms and raced down the hall toward his office. "Y'all, go ahead, we have a *detour* to take before the awards. We'll Uber and meet you there."

Once they were inside Ben's office, his entire being changed. Lowering her feet to the floor, he didn't speak, instead he backed her into his desk until it halted them both. Ben's eyes held an intensity she'd never witnessed before. His hands dropped to her stomach and his gaze followed.

Involuntarily, Ray's hands landed on top of his and her attention was glued to their hands, as was his. When Ben finally spoke, his words were rough with emotions and directed at their hands.

"You know how many times I've lain awake at night just looking at the contrast of us?" He wasn't really speaking to her. "Too many to count." For a while the sounds of their breathing were all that broke the silence.

"Me too." It was a confession she never thought she'd make. Especially since, more often than not, it was prompted by an ignorant or hateful comment she'd overheard or directed right at them. Their difference never bothered her, even when people got hateful. Those people had the opposite impact than they intended. It made her love everything about *them* that much more.

"Now, we've made a child. A perfect child. One full of contrast. The world won't change him, no, he'll change the world." Ben's words were simple, but the emotion and unspoken vow was not.

A shiver wracked her body as Ben's hands slipped around her waist. His fingertips whispered up the skin at the open back of her dress. Something wicked flashed behind his eyes and he bit that damn lower lip. Rayna groaned aloud as heat pooled in naughty places.

"Turn around and bend over." Ben swiped the desk clear with one muscular forearm. "This is going to be fast and rough, then we have a ceremony to attend before I can do it all over again, but in Arizona."

Ben spun her around, lowering just her chest to the mahogany surface. The coolness of the wood seeped through the thin satin of her dress. Her nipples pebbled as she heard Ben fumbling with his pants.

Without ceremony, his hands were under the skirt of her dress and he pulled her thong to the side. One long finger dragged slowly through her wetness, ripping a strangled moan from her. "Ben, please?"

Before the last syllable left her lips, Ben was buried inside her. "God, I fucking love you, Cookie." Ben pounded into her, giving her no quarter, not that she wanted any. "Thanks for giving us a second chance." His arms wound around her body and gently cradled her stomach.

His rough fucking and tender touch was maddening. *Talk about contrasts.* All thought fled as her muscles started to contract with pleasure.

Her words were stilted in time with his thrusts. "I fucking love you too, and thanks for taking this detour. . .with me." She panted, throwing his joking word back at him.

"Come, Ray. Fuuuuuck." The word was drawn out. "Your pussy is magic, but I need you to fucking come...now." The combination of his cock and his command had her orgasm crashing over her in no time. A few strokes and Ben followed her.

Their bodies still connected, Ben dropped forward and whispered. "Anytime, babe." He bit her earlobe. "Unexpected detours are the best part of the journey."

DEAR READER

Thank you for reading *Second Chance Detour*.

You may have read it under another title before the changes and added scene.

If you enjoyed this tale, please consider leaving a review of Second Chance Detour and checking out my other books.

PLAYLIST

This is the playlist the characters in this book "shared" with me as theirs. I listened to this music while writing the book to connect with them.

Listen on Spotify. https://smarturl.it/SCDPlaylist

NO endorsement by the artists or their representatives is given or implied by sharing this list. I hold no rights to any music/song listed here.

ACKNOWLEDGMENTS

Take everyone I've ever mentioned in this section in previous books and amplify it. The village who make my books better, I love you all.

Thanks to Amber (& Angie), Megan, Sam, and likely a few other people I forgot to shout-out who helped me re-brand, re-title, re-blurb, re-release, and other res, this story.

Wander and Andrey, smooches for just being y'all and for your generosity that made this cover smoking hot. I love you both to pieces.

My Facebook friends and followers, y'all always come through when I ask a question or need help, with say, car breakdowns in the name of research.

I want to thank everyone who has ever shared something I posted, liked something I shared, or just sat back and laughed at a meme that cracks them up. Social media wouldn't be the same without you.

My family, as always, you are my anchor on stormy seas...and also the stormy seas, but it makes for interesting sailing. Yeah, are all these nautical references doing it for you? Me neither, love you all.

Vixens, you make my life better, period.

Lastly, if you feel like I should have mentioned you here, I damn well should have but always fuck up and forget, so thanks...insert name here...for...insert reason here...even though I forgot you here, I will never truly forget you. If you impacted me, you are in my heart, but I just don't always look in the right place. Thanks for being you and not being pissed that I didn't get your name in. Next time, I'll do better.

ALSO BY VERLENE

ANTHOLOGIES

Vegas Strong
(Charity: The Code Green Campaign)

AUDIO

Ryder Hard

ORDERED SERIES
(best read in order)

Desert Phantoms MC
*The Black Stetson $^{DPMC\,.5}$
Thunder $^{DPMC\,1}$
Trip $^{DPMC\,1}$

Shadow Angels MC
Crossing Styx $^{SAMC\,1}$

Imagine Ink
*(*temporarily unpublished*)*

STAND-ALONE

Beckon
ABCs of Love

Control Line
Everyday Heroes World

Dangerous Curve Ahead
On the Road to Love

DIY Hearts
#LoveHack

Exit the Friend Zone
On the Road to Love

Ryder Hard

Second Chance Detour
On the Road to Love

The Black Stetson
Desert Phantoms MC .5

Unveiled
The Salvation Society

*The Black Stetson is the unofficial prequel to Desert Phantoms MC. It does NOT need to be read to start the series but is the back story of Bullseye and the introduction of some of the brothers.

ABOUT VERLENE

Verlene was born and raised in the south, and pens smoking hot tales of life, lust, and love.

Thanks to the military, she's traveled the US but now calls Sin City home...again.

A self-proclaimed zombie apocalypse enthusiast, word porn peddler, human canvas, Manowarrior, serial grammar killer, rabid Bama fan, accidental dust bunny population specialist, and Harley riding, abuser of the word f*ck. A lover of all things Lemmy, wine, skulls, and the 80s.

She's thrown live grenades, survived the tear gas chamber, and forced road marches but still believes writing and self-publishing are more brutal.

Verlene's current published works include contemporary romance series, anthology contributions, sci-fi romance, and several stand-alone reads with various contemporary themes. Look for exciting new releases from her in paranormal, MFM, and who knows what else.

Verlene is on a mission to make naughty the new normal, one book at a time.

* * *

If you want to stay up to date on my latest releases & happenings...

- Subscribe to my newsletter. www.smarturl.it/VLNews
- Text Alerts – Text MyNextBBF to (725) 241-5683
- Follow me on Amazon & Bookbub. Verlene Landon

If you like a healthy dose of naughty fun, giveaways, and sneak peeks at upcoming books before anyone else, join my Facebook reader group, Verlene's Vixens

- www.facebook.com/groups/VerleneLandon

I love to connect with readers, so feel free to use any of my links to find me online.

- Facebook Page: Author Verlene Landon
- Facebook Profile: Verlene Landon
- Instagram: Verlene.Landon
- Twitter: Verlene_Landon
- TikTok: Author_VerleneLandon
- Email: Verlene.Landon@gmail.com
- Signed Books & Merchandise:
- verlenelandon.com/books-merch
- These links & more can be found at www.VerleneLandon.com/links